RODDY DOYLE

Illustrated by EMILY HUGHES

AMULET BOOKS
NEW YORK

Brilliant

Library of Congress Cataloging-in-Publication Data

Doyle, Roddy, 1958–
Brilliant / by Roddy Doyle ; illustrated by Emily Hughes.
pages cm
"First published in the United Kingdom in 2014 by Macmillan Children's Books."
ISBN 978-1-4197-1479-5
[1. Depression, Mental—Fiction. 2. Adventure and adventurers—Fiction. 3. Brothers and sisters—Fiction. 4. Magic—Fiction. 5. Dogs—Fiction. 6. Animals—Fiction. 7. Dublin (Ireland)—Fiction. 8. Ireland—Fiction.] I. Hughes, Emily (Emily M.), illustrator. II. Title.
PZ7.D7773Bri 2015
[Fic]—dc23
2014040996

First published in the United Kingdom in 2014 by
Macmillan Children's Books.

Printed and bound in U.S.A.
10 9 8 7 6 5 4 3 2 1

ABRAMS
THE ART OF BOOKS SINCE 1949
115 West 18th Street
New York, NY 10011
www.abramsbooks.com

TO DUBLIN'S
SEAGULLS

The Black Dog came in the night.

He came in a cloud—he was the cloud. A huge cloud that covered the city.
And the city—the air above the city—became even darker. For just a while.
Then the black cloud got smaller, and smaller. Until it was a small cloud that
sank lower to the ground, and its shape became doglike and the doglike shape
became a dog.

The Black Dog of Depression had invaded the city of Dublin.

But no one noticed.

No humans noticed.

But the animals did.

The city's pets tried to warn their owners, but the humans weren't listen-
ing. A bark was a bark, and a meow was just a meow.

The Black Dog had arrived. He crept through the city's streets. He slid
along the shadows and made no noise at all. He slid and crept, and sneaked
into houses and flats—wherever he could find the humans.

The city's dogs hated what was happening.

Dublin loved dogs. And the city's dogs knew they were lucky.

"All this food and water!" said a dog called Sadie. "Oh my God! And all I have to do, like, is wag my tail and remember to pee and, like, poo in the garden."

"I forget sometimes," said a second dog, called Chester.

"Me too, like," said Sadie.

"The only thing I have to do," said Chester, "is pretend I'm happy when my owner comes home from work."

"Do you have to pretend?" Sadie asked.

"Sometimes," said Chester.

"Oh my God," said Sadie. "I never do."

"Aren't you great?" said Chester, a bit sarcastically. (Dogs, especially Dublin dogs, can be very sarcastic. Just listen very carefully to the barks, especially early in the morning.)

The dogs knew: There was only one way to stop the Black Dog of Depression. But all they could do was watch as the Black Dog started to prowl in the night and move in closer to the humans. It was horrible to see how he could become part of the air and slide into houses. How he could change the mood, kill laughter, and wipe smiles from faces that had been smiling for years. How he could change sleep from a pleasant dream into a nightmare.

The two dogs, Chester and Sadie, lived very near each other. They were almost next-door neighbors. There was only one house between theirs, and it belonged to a man called Ben Kelly. They both liked Ben. He didn't have a dog of his own, but he always treated them well whenever he saw them going for a walk or barking at him from inside their houses. They both liked sitting on the backs of the couches in their front rooms.

"Oh my God!" said Sadie. "Do you do that as well?"

"I do, yeah," said Chester.

"That's, like, amazing!" said Sadie.

"Passes the time." Chester shrugged.

Ben lived alone, but there were always people coming and going. There was always music and laughter. And there were two children that the dogs liked. Two kids who used to come to Ben's house. They called him Uncle Ben.

"What's an uncle?" Sadie asked Chester.

"Don't know," Chester admitted. "But I think it might have something to do with chips."

"Chips?"

"Yeah," said Chester. "He buys them chips whenever they come to the house."

The children, a boy and a girl, loved their Uncle Ben. And, it was clear, Ben loved them. But then the Black Dog slid into Ben's house—and hundreds, thousands, of other houses. He came at night, hiding in the darkness.

Dogs, and most other animals, love the nighttime. It's the time when they can be themselves, when they can do most of their barking and howling. They're not expected to wag their tails forever or to fetch sticks and stupid plastic toys. People go to bed, and their pets can secretly relax. It's a magic time, when the daylight rules wobble and the humans don't notice things as much. Unusual events seem normal or don't get noticed. Two talking dogs might actually be two human voices carried in the wind. A black dog–shaped shadow creeping up the stairs is probably the moon behind the tree outside in the front garden.

It made the city's animals angry that the Black Dog used the night to spread his poison. But they knew: There was nothing that Sadie or Chester or any of the city's other dogs and pets could do to stop him.

Only the city's kids could do that.

CHAPTER I

Gloria Kelly lay in bed. She was wide awake. And she knew her brother, Raymond, was too. She could tell by the way he was breathing. It was awake breath. He was lying there, thinking and listening. Sleep breath was different. It was longer and lighter, less in and out.

"Rayzer?" she whispered.

Raymond didn't answer. But she didn't care.

She liked sharing the bedroom. Although she knew Raymond didn't. But she didn't care about that, either. She could like it in secret. She didn't have to tell him.

She'd been moved into Raymond's room when their Uncle Ben had come to live with them. For a while. That was what her mam and dad had said. Uncle Ben would be staying "for a while." Sometimes her mother called it "a little while." But the "little" had disappeared when Uncle Ben kept staying, and

Gloria began to think that her bedroom wasn't hers anymore.
And Raymond, she supposed, began to think the same thing.
His room had become *their* room.

She looked into her room sometimes, when her Uncle
Ben wasn't in there. He hadn't done anything to it. He hadn't
touched her pictures or her other stuff. It was still pink, nearly
everything in it. The only really new thing in the room was
her Uncle Ben's smell. It was kind of an adult smell. A mixture
of soap and sweatiness. There were none of his clothes lying
around, and just one book that wasn't hers. She'd looked at the
cover, but it had looked boring, about a war or something. Except for the fact that she didn't sleep or play in there anymore,

6

it was still Gloria's room. So maybe her Uncle Ben really was only staying for a while—but the while was a bit longer than they'd expected.

Maybe.

"Rayzer?"

He still wouldn't answer.

She didn't like her bed. It wasn't a real bed. It was just a mattress on the floor. She'd liked it at first. It had been fun, nearly like camping. But not now. Her face was sometimes right against the wall, low down, at the baseboard, nearly where it joined the floor. It was cold there. Always—even when the rest of the room was warm. And she could hear things sometimes— she thought she could. Behind the baseboard.

Gloria wished she had her own bed. That was all she missed, really. She had her duvet and her pink cover. But it wasn't the same.

"Rayzer?"

She said it a bit louder. Nearly her regular talking voice.

Maybe he was asleep. She kind of liked that, the fact that her big brother had fallen asleep before her.

She tried again.

"Rayzer?"

"What?"

"Are you not asleep?"

"That's a stupid question."

"I bet you were asleep," said Gloria. "And I woke you."

"I wasn't," said Raymond.

"Bet you were," said Gloria. "Prove it."

"Easy," said Raymond. "You said 'Rayzer' four times."

She heard him moving, turning in his bed.

"Didn't you?"

"Yeah," she said. "I think. Why didn't you answer?"

"Didn't want to."

"I knew that," said Gloria. "I knew you were awake."

"What d'you want?"

"Can you hear them?" said Gloria.

"Yeah."

Gloria was talking about the grown-ups downstairs. Her mam, her dad, her granny, and Uncle Ben. They were downstairs in the kitchen. Raymond's bedroom was right on top of them.

"They're mumbling again," Gloria whispered.

"Yeah," said Raymond.

The house was full of mumbles these days. Mumbles that often stopped whenever Raymond or Gloria walked into the room. Mumbling was what grown-ups did when they thought they were whispering. Whispers only stayed in the air for a little while, but mumbles rolled around for ages, in the high corners, along the window frames, all around the house. The mumbles had almost become creatures. Gloria imagined she could see them. They were made of dust and hair, pushed into a ball, with skinny legs that barely touched the walls and ceilings as they slid along the paint and glass and wood.

The mumbling had started when their Uncle Ben had come to live with them. Or just before he came. Gloria didn't like the mumbles. They worried her. But she didn't blame her Uncle Ben for them.

Neither did Raymond. He didn't like having to share his bedroom with Gloria, but he didn't blame his Uncle Ben for that, either. Gloria was a pain in the neck—and in other places too.

But Raymond knew all little sisters were like that. It was one of the rules of life. And sometimes sharing the bedroom wasn't too bad. Like now. Raymond had always been a bit afraid of the dark. Just a small bit. He was nearly two years older than Gloria, so he went to bed half an hour after her. It was a quarter of an hour for each year. That was the rule, his dad had told him.

"Who made the rule?" Raymond had asked his dad.

"The government," his dad had answered.

His dad thought he was funny.

Anyway, when Raymond had gone up to bed, he'd always left his bedroom door open a bit, so that light from the kitchen downstairs could get in and push away some of the darkness. He'd always hated it when he saw Gloria's door closed, with her stupid sign: "Keep Out—This Means U!!!" Because Gloria wasn't scared of the dark. And that had made Raymond feel terrible, and ashamed.

But now, with Gloria sharing the bedroom, Raymond wasn't really scared of the dark anymore. And he didn't have to say anything about it, or be grateful or anything. It was just a fact.

"Mumble, mumble, mumble," said Gloria, now.

Raymond did a deep, man mumble.

"Mummm-bull."

Gloria did a lady one.

"Mimm-bill, mimm-bill. Know what we should do, Rayzer?"

"What?"

"Sneak down, under the table."

"Cool."

It was the night before Saint Patrick's Day. There was no school the next day, and they'd already been allowed to stay up later than usual.

Gloria heard Raymond getting out of his bed. She stood up on her mattress.

Gloria and Raymond had this secret thing, a game. They'd sneak back downstairs—only on the weekends—after they'd been sent to bed, and only when the grown-ups were in the kitchen. It didn't really work in the other rooms. They'd sneak down the stairs and along the hall. They'd creep into the kitchen on their hands and knees or sliding along on their bellies. They'd crawl in under the table, and they'd stay there. For as long as they could.

They couldn't touch the adult feet or they'd be caught and the game would end and they'd be sent back up to bed. The first time they did it, they'd only lasted two minutes and fourteen seconds because their dad moved his foot and felt something.

"There's a dog under the table," he said. "But we don't have a dog."

Then they saw his big face, upside down, looking at them.

"Messers," he said. "Get back up to bed."

And their mam grabbed and tickled them when they were climbing out from under.

"You scamps!"

It became something they did nearly every Friday and Saturday night. It was brilliant, because their parents always forgot. And their granny—she forgot too. But their granny forgot nearly everything, so she didn't really count.

But one night, when they were under the table for thirty-seven minutes and fifty-one seconds, Raymond and Gloria realized something at the exact same time: Their parents knew they were there. They were in on the game. In fact, it had become *their* game: Pretending they didn't know their kids were under the table. Their parents owned the game, not Gloria and Raymond.

It was the way their mam and dad were talking to each other—that was the giveaway. And what they were saying.

"Here, Pat," said their mam. "You know the way Gloria and Raymond are asleep in bed?"

"I do," said their dad.

"Well," said their mam. "Will we eat the chocolate we hid in the secret place where they'd never, ever find it?"

"Good idea," said their dad. "They'll never know."

It wasn't funny, and not because Gloria thought there was a hiding place for chocolate that she'd never found. (She didn't.)

11

What wasn't funny was the fact that the game was over—Raymond and Gloria had been caught. And, actually, they might have been caught ages ago but they hadn't noticed. Their parents, even their granny, had been playing with them, like three cats with two mice.

Raymond and Gloria got out from under the table.

"Oh, look," said their mam.

"Were you under the table?" said their dad.

"All the time?" said their mam.

"Ha, ha," said Raymond. "I don't think."

Gloria had cried. She hadn't meant to. Her parents never really teased her. But it felt like they'd been teasing her for ages—forever—and she'd only just found out. She hated being teased. She hated it.

Her parents knew they'd gone too far, and they felt guilty. Gloria sat on her dad's lap while her mam made them all hot chocolate.

"Time for bed," said their mam when the chocolate was finished.

Gloria's dad kissed the top of Gloria's head, then Raymond's.

"You can sneak under the table any time you want," he said.

"Yes," said their mam.

But they didn't.

Not for ages.

Weeks. Months. Nearly a year.

Their parents missed it—Raymond and Gloria could tell.

"Make sure you stay in bed now," said their dad, the next Friday night.

They stayed in bed.

"No sneaking under the table tonight," he said the following night.

They stayed in bed.

"Did you fall asleep last night?" their dad asked Raymond on Sunday morning.

"I fall asleep every night," said Raymond. "Can you pass the milk, please?"

Raymond and Gloria both agreed. They'd never sneak downstairs again—until they knew the game was theirs again.

They even forgot about the game.

Then one day, a few days after Christmas, Gloria was in the kitchen and she dropped one of the charms from the new bracelet her granny had given her. It fell under the table, and Gloria went in after it. And she remembered.

She said nothing until she was alone with Raymond.

"Hey, Rayzer," she said.

"What?"

He was playing tennis against himself on his new Wii.

"Remember when we used to go under the table?" said Gloria.

"Oh yeah!"

And they started again.

That night, they crept down the stairs, down the hall, into the kitchen, under the table. They stayed there when their parents and their granny stood up. They stayed when they heard their parents going up the stairs. And they waited.

"They'll catch us if they look into our rooms before they go to bed," Gloria whispered.

They listened.

They heard the toilet. They heard the water going on, and off. They heard a cough, and gargling. They heard a laugh— their mother. They heard silence.

"They didn't check."

They'd won.

And they won again, and again—and again. They crept and they slid, and they were sure their parents never knew. The best bit, the biggest triumph, was sitting under the table. For minutes. For more and more minutes. They stayed absolutely still. But it was hard. Their noses got runny, their ears got itchy. Burps climbed slowly up their throats and knocked at their teeth to get out. Their legs and bums went numb, then dead, then back to jumpy life. They bit their arms to stop laughing.

It went on for months.

And it got even better when their Uncle Ben arrived. Now they had to slide through four sets of feet and legs. Being under the table was like being in a cage, and the grown-up legs were like the iron bars. But these iron bars wore slippers or had holes in their socks, and some of them even had hair in the gaps between the socks and trousers. So it was funny—especially once, when Raymond leaned out and pretended he was going to pull one of the black hairs on their dad's shin. There were the legs of the table too, and the chairs. They made the secret space under the table even more like a cage.

Sometimes Gloria didn't like being small. But sometimes it was great, like when she was able to slide between the legs and sit with her hair just touching the underside of the table. Sometimes, when the grown-ups were drinking tea, she thought she could feel the heat from a cup coming through the table, on top of her head. It was nice, like a friendly hand. It made her feel relaxed, even when her legs were stiff and her mam's knee was only a millimeter away from the tip of Gloria's nose.

There was another thing about their Uncle Ben coming to stay. The grown-ups spent much more time sitting in the kitchen. Chatting, talking—and mumbling.

Chatting was when they were telling one another what they'd done that day, or what they were planning for the next day.

"Add Krispies to the list there. Is there anything worth watching on TV?"

"Your man is on."

"Who?"

"That fella who used to be on the other thing. The fella with the hair. You know him."

"I don't."

"Ah, you do."

"I don't. What about his hair?"

"It's not his. It's a rug."

"Oh, him?"

"Who?"

"I'm not watching him."

"Who?"

Who? was their granny's favorite word. Followed by *What?*

"Add butter to the list too, love. We're running out."

"What?"

"I'll tell you who has a rug, closer to home. You know your man who's going with my cousin Rita?"

"That's not a wig, is it?"

"It is, yeah."

"It's not."

"It is."

"Who?"

"How do you know it's a wig?"

"Gerry from work told me."

"How does he know?"

"Who?"

"He grew up with him. The same road. He was bald for about five years before the wig arrived."

"No."

"What?"

"Well, that's what Paddy says."

"Who?"

That was chatting. It was boring, but sometimes funny, sometimes deliberately funny, but most times accidentally. Chatting and laughing usually went together.

Talking was like chatting, but a bit more serious. It was often about work, or money, or things that were happening in Ireland and the world.

"We don't need them."

"What?"

"But they're nice. You can't have a cup of tea without a biscuit."

"Yes, you can. It's easy, look."

"Ah, now, we'd be in a bad way if we couldn't have a biscuit with tea."

"It doesn't have to be these ones. There are cheaper biscuits."

"I like these ones."

Sometimes, Gloria and Raymond couldn't tell if they were listening to talking or chatting. It was often hard to tell. A chat about the price of biscuits became a conversation about how people were having difficulty paying for all sorts of things—houses, clothes, heating—and about how the government was doing nothing. They weren't chatting anymore. They were talking.

Then something would happen.

"Well, at least we have our health."

"That's true."

"Speaking of health. Did you see the state of your man next door? He has a belly on him that'd stop the tide from coming in."

"And she's thin as a rake."

They'd be chatting again, and whatever they'd been talking about was forgotten.

"That's often the way, isn't it? Fat fella, skinny girl."

"Or the other way round. Big girls aren't exactly an endangered species."

"What?"

When their granny said *Who?* or *What?*, one of her dog slippers always jumped a bit, like it was talking too. It was really funny.

Sometimes, without Raymond or Gloria noticing—they were busy trying not to laugh or groan—the chatting would swerve back to talking. Talking often came with sighs and *I don't knows*.

"We'll stay at home this year, will we?"

"Here? In the house, like?"

"We can go somewhere different every day. It'll be nice."

"It could end up being as expensive as going somewhere for the two weeks."

"Not really. If we're careful."

"I don't know . . ."

"It'll be grand."

"Ah, sure, Dublin's great."

That was their granny. Her slippers were jumping up and down.

"Sure, they come from all over the world to see Dublin."

"God love them. Did I say sugar?"

"What?"

"On the list. Sugar. Is it there?"

"What?"

"Sugar."

"Who?"

Then there was mumbling.

Now, the night before Saint Patrick's Day, as Gloria very carefully opened the bedroom door, they could hear the mumbling coming from downstairs.

"Mimm-bill, mimm-bill," she whispered.

"Mummm-bull," Raymond whispered back.

Mumbling was different. Chatting often changed into talking, and back to chatting. But mumbling was always mumbling. It was like a foreign language, heard through walls and floors.

Gloria held the door handle down as far as it would go. She pressed her other hand flat against the door as she pulled it open. This stopped the hinges from groaning. She opened the door slowly but without stopping or hesitating.

Raymond and Gloria didn't like the mumbling. They didn't understand it. But one thing about it was clear: Mumbling was very serious. There was never any laughter mixed in with it.

They were on the landing now, about to creep down the stairs. They knew the stairs by heart. They knew the bumps and squeaks of every step. They could have gone up and down with their eyes shut and not holding the banister. Actually, they did that quite a lot—because they'd been told not to. It was brilliant. Especially going down. And they did it for practice, so it would be perfect when they were sneaking down at night. There was only one really loud step, the second one from the bottom. The noise it made—a long spooky metally groan—was caused by a loose nail under the carpet. They knew this because every time he heard the groan their dad would say, "That nail's on my list for the weekend." He'd been saying it all their lives. Or sometimes, "That nail's on my list," or just, "That's on the list."

It was a family joke. If any of them heard a groan, they'd say, "That's on the list." It didn't have to be a stair. Anything that groaned, they said it. A metal gate, a wooden bench. They even said it when they heard a human groan.

Their Uncle Ben had fractured two of his ribs a few years before he'd come to live with them. He wasn't wrapped in bandages, but he had to take it easy, stay in his house, and do nothing. So they'd gone to visit him with some DVDs and grapes.

"I'm grand, I'm grand," he kept saying.

But he'd groaned when he was sitting down.

"That's on the list," said their mam. "Oh God, sorry, Ben."

They'd all started laughing, including Uncle Ben, even though laughing was agony for him, and even funnier—and even more agony.

There was only one big groan, but every step had its own

20

small noises. Sometimes it felt like the stairs were a bit human. It was like walking down a nice giant, from the top of his head to his feet. He'd sigh and moan as they went, and then the last big groan on the second step—it was like the giant was pretending he was going to stand up and chase them down the hall.

Now, they stepped right over the second step, first Gloria, then Raymond, so they wouldn't wake the giant. But it was tricky. They had to make sure they didn't put too much weight on the last step, because it had its own little squeak. If they went too quickly or went right over the last step, their feet would make too much noise when they landed on the hall floor.

They were there now, in the hall. So far, so good. They listened. The mumbles were still coming from the kitchen. No one had heard them. Mission accomplished—so far. It was eight steps to the kitchen door. These were easy to do because there were no squeaky floorboards. Gloria and Raymond could walk quietly over the rug. But there was one big problem. The kitchen door was always open.

They got down on the floor and started to slide.

They didn't mind things being serious. They knew that not everything could be funny. Laughing was only good when it was a bit of a surprise. They hated people who laughed all the time. They had an auntie called Deirdre who laughed at everything.

"Good morning."

"Good morning—HAHAHAHAHAHAH!"

She laughed at absolutely everything.

"We've no milk."

"No milk—HAHAHAHAHAHAH!"

They hated her. They didn't hate *her*. But they hated when she laughed and she never stopped, so it was hard not to hate her a bit too. She always called Gloria "Glory-Be-to-God."

"How's Glory-Be-to-God—HAHAHAHAHAH?"

"It's her nerves," their granny told them once, after Auntie Deirdre had laughed when Raymond told her that his goldfish had died. "She's always been a bit nervous," their granny explained. "She didn't mean to be cruel. Here."

Here was their favorite granny word. It meant she was bending over to get her purse from her handbag, to give them money for sweets. Their mam called it bribery and she didn't like it.

"You're spoiling them."

Raymond and Gloria agreed, but they loved it. Their granny agreed too, but she didn't care.

"Ah, now, a bit of bribery never hurt anyone," she always said.

Anyway, Raymond and Gloria knew there was more to life than laughing. When chatting turned into talking, when the grown-ups started getting serious—they didn't mind that. They knew that food and clothes cost money, and that holidays cost money, and the thing that their parents spoke about as if it was a snake getting ready to bite, the mortgage. They knew about the recession, even though they didn't know exactly what it was. They watched the news sometimes with their parents, even though it was boring. But their parents liked them to watch it.

"You'll remember this," said Gloria's mam as they watched people celebrating in Egypt.

"Why will I?" Gloria asked.

"You just will," said her mam.

Gloria was snuggled in beside her.

"It's a big event," said her mam. "A revolution."

Her mam was probably right. Gloria saw things on the news, like the tsunami in Japan, and she knew she'd remember them for the rest of her life. Because they were often so scary and terrible. Or mad—like the woman throwing the cat into the trash bin in England. Gloria would never forget that.

But most of the news was about banks and politicians and

people shouting, and the recession and the euro, and men who were older than their dad saying, "Let me explain. It's quite simple."

Gloria and Raymond knew it wasn't simple and that sometimes chatting had to become talking. And they didn't mind—because they were allowed to listen. There was nothing secret about it. The times were hard, and their mam and dad wanted them to know that.

They had to creep now, slither along the last bit of the hall, so no one in kitchen would see them. The kitchen door was always open. But never wide open. If they stayed on the floor, and if all the adults were sitting at the table, they could wriggle around the door and across the floor without being seen.

Raymond looked first. He waited, then stuck his head around the open door. They were all sitting down. He started to slide, and Gloria followed him.

Mumbling was different. Mumbling was private. The grown-ups only mumbled when they didn't want the kids to hear what they were saying. Gloria and Raymond hated it. It wasn't fair and it frightened them—a bit. But mostly it annoyed them.

They loved their Uncle Ben, but the mumbling had started just before he'd come to stay.

Gloria was following Raymond. Her face was nearly touching the soles of his feet. He was fast, but the really amazing thing was, she couldn't hear him. He could wriggle across the kitchen like an eel she'd once seen on TV moving through water.

There was a space at the end of the table, between Uncle

Ben's boots and their granny's slippers. Raymond only needed a second. Gloria didn't have to wait—she was right behind him. He slid in between the feet and sat up, under the table, and crossed his legs in tight. He did all this in what looked like one slick movement. And so did Gloria. Just like a seal—Gloria thought—sliding onto a rock in the zoo.

They sat there now, under the kitchen table, and waited.

CHAPTER 2

W e've a bit of news for you," said Gloria's mam.

Gloria should have known. They'd just had ice cream—in the middle of the week. It had been a trap. She knew that now. She looked at Raymond, and he knew it too.

The ice cream was gone. They couldn't taste it anymore. "We've a bit of news for you." It was going to be bad. News was nearly always bad. There was the time their mam had told them their granddad had died. There was the time their dad had told them that their cat, Cecil, had gone away and wouldn't be coming back. And here they were, full of chicken and chocolate chip ice cream, about to be given more bad news, again.

Gloria glared at her mam.

"What?" said her mam.

"What?" said her granny.

"Mam," said Gloria. "I hate surprises. You know that."

"Even nice ones?" said her mam.

Gloria didn't answer. She wasn't going to play their game. Her mam and dad would just have to tell them the news. Gloria wasn't going to help them.

"So anyway," said their mam. "Do you want to tell them?" she asked their dad.

Raymond and Gloria knew it now, for sure. The news was going to be terrible.

"Okay," said their dad. "Well—"

He stopped. He scratched his chin.

"Your Uncle Ben is coming to stay for a while."

They didn't really hear him. They were so ready for something bad, they didn't actually hear the words or understand them properly.

"What?" said Gloria, just before her granny said it.

"Your Uncle Ben is coming to stay," said their dad. "For a while."

It still took a few seconds for it to mean anything. It was like Gloria and Raymond could see each of their dad's words, like a stream of little clouds across the kitchen, just beneath the ceiling. They had to examine each word again, one by one, until they got to *stay*.

Then they understood.

And they went mad. Gloria charged for the back door—she had to scream her happiness. Then she changed her mind—she had to hug her parents. Then she screamed anyway—because she couldn't not scream.

"Oh, Mother of God!" her granny screamed back.

"She hears when she wants to," said Gloria's dad, to her mam.

"Ah, come on," said her mam. "Dead people in Russia could hear that scream."

"What?" said their granny.

Gloria hugged her granny.

"I'm not really deaf," her granny whispered. "It's just more interesting when I am. Shhhhh."

The "Shhhhh" went straight into Gloria's ear and made her laugh even more. It was hot in the kitchen by the time they all calmed down.

Gloria sat on her dad's lap.

This had happened more than two months before Saint Patrick's Day, just after they'd gone back to school after Christmas.

"When's he coming?" Raymond asked.

"The weekend," said his dad. "Probably. It'll be for a while, just."

Their Uncle Ben didn't live far away, in another country or anything—like their Uncle Derek, who lived in Australia. Raymond and Gloria had only ever met their Uncle Derek once. But Ben only lived about ten minutes away.

"Yes," said their mam. "Just a little while. Till he sorts things out."

There was a silence then—one of those short, important silences. Gloria couldn't see her dad's face, but she could see her mam looking at her dad, and she knew that her dad was looking back at her mam. Gloria thought her mam had probably said something she hadn't meant to, but Gloria didn't know what it was. She was in the silly, secret world of adults and she didn't want to be. So she looked at her mam and asked her.

"What does that mean?"

"What does what—" her mam started, then stopped. She smiled, and started again: "You mean, what did I mean when I said, 'Till he sorts things out'?"

"Yeah."

Gloria knew about divorce and stuff. But Uncle Ben wasn't married and Gloria didn't think he had a girlfriend. She always checked whenever she was in Ben's house. She looked for women's magazines or clothes, or extra stuff in the fridge.

"Well," said her mam. "Ben's business is struggling a bit."

"The recession," said Raymond.

"That's right," said their mam, and she smiled.

Parents loved it when their kids used important words.

"So," said their dad. "He can't really afford his house."

"But it's his," said Gloria.

"Yes, but."

Gloria could feel her dad sitting up.

"This house," he said. "It's ours. We own it. Me and Una."

Una was their mam. Their dad's name was Pat.

"What about us?" said Gloria. "We own it as well, don't we?"

"Well, yes," said their dad, and he kissed the top of her head. "But, no."

They laughed—her mam, her dad, her deaf granny. But Gloria and Raymond didn't.

29

"Strictly speaking," said their dad, "legally speaking—the law, like—myself and your mam own it. It's in our names, as they say."

"Who's they?"

"The banks and the lawyers and that," said her dad. "But so, anyway. We got a loan from the bank—it's called a mortgage—to buy the house. Because you could never save enough to do it. It's not like buying something in J. C. Penney's."

Raymond groaned.

"What's wrong?"

"I'm not stupid," said Raymond.

"Neither am I," Gloria told Raymond.

"I'm just explaining," said their dad.

"Okay."

"Anyway," said their dad. "We have to pay back the loan, the mortgage, like, a bit every month."

"Is it much?"

"We can manage," said their dad.

"We're grand," said their mam.

"I've my job and Una has hers, so we're fine," said their dad. "Even though Una isn't working as much as she used to."

"It's grand," said their mam.

She worked in a supermarket near where they lived. There'd been a meeting about a month before, and the manager had told the staff that business was down—although they'd known that already. They'd all decided to work fewer hours instead of some of them losing their jobs. Their mam had said they'd all been crying, even the manager. But the funny thing was, it had been the best meeting she'd ever been at, even though she'd be earning less money and the shop might still have to close down.

"It was just, we're all friends," she'd said. "And it was nice to know what that means."

"So," said their dad now. "We pay money to the bank every month."

Gloria was getting worried. The adults talked about money like they talked about sickness.

"Anyway," said their mam. "Ben."

"Yeah," said their dad. "Ben. Ben's mortgage has become too steep—too expensive, like. And the bank isn't being very nice about it. So."

"He's coming to live with us."

"Yeah."

"Cool."

"But," said Raymond. "Can he not live in his own house anymore?"

"No," said their dad. "He can't. That's the thing."

"It's very unfair," said their mam.

"It's rough," said their dad.

"The poor lad," said their granny.

"But it's his house," said Gloria.

"Yes, it is," said her dad. "But—"

He kind of slumped. He was resting his chin on Gloria's head. It was nice.

He sighed.

"It's happening to loads of people," he said.

31

"But anyway," said their mam. "He's coming to stay here and that's nice, isn't it?"

"Yeah!"

"And," said their mam.

It was one of her big announcement "And"s.

"He'll have to have a room of his own," she said. "Won't he?"

Raymond and Gloria said nothing. They were working it out. There were three bedrooms in the house. Their parents had the biggest one. And their granny lived in her granny-flat. It had its own front door and it used to be the garage, before their granny came to live with them—before Gloria could remember. So that left one of their bedrooms. Raymond's. Or Gloria's.

"Gloria."

"Why not Raymond?"

"I haven't finished yet," said her mam. "So don't be rude, please."

"Sorry."

"That's okay, love," said her mam. "It's going to be a bit of a squash. And your room is smaller than Raymond's. So you'll be moving in with him."

Raymond and Gloria looked at each other. They didn't like this, but they quickly remembered the better news: Uncle Ben was coming to stay.

"Okay," said Raymond.

"Okay," said Gloria.

"It'll be nice," said their mam.

"Yeah," said Gloria, and she meant it.

• • •

Uncle Ben arrived the next Saturday with his stuff in his van. They all helped him bring it into the house and they brought some of it up to Gloria's room. His suitcase and a cardboard box.

Gloria looked in the box when she was putting it on the bed. There were a couple of books and loads of CDs, and a bottle of stuff called Old Spice, and a lamp for beside the bed. The bedclothes had been changed. Her pink cover and pillowcase were over in Raymond's room, and the covers were blue now. It made Gloria a bit sad, even a tiny bit annoyed. But then she heard Uncle Ben and her dad laughing downstairs, and she ran down to see what had happened.

Her dad was standing in the hall with another cardboard box. But the bottom of it had split open, so he was holding an empty box and the things that had been in it were all around him on the ground and on top of his feet.

"You're an eejit," said Uncle Ben.

"I know," said her dad.

He bent down and started picking up Uncle Ben's stuff. Gloria helped him. There were old football medals, loads of them. The ribbons were all tangled, so they looked like some sort of mad doll's head, with braids with coins in them.

"I'll untangle them for you, Uncle Ben," she said.

"Thanks, Gloria," said Uncle Ben. "It'll take you all day."

"Bet it won't," said Gloria.

But it did. She spent most of the rest of the day untangling the ribbons. She made sure she didn't pull any, so the knots wouldn't get tighter. It was dark when she loosened the last knot. The ribbon must have been really old because the medal with it—"Community Games Runner-Up"—had "1989" on it. So her Uncle Ben had won it twenty-four years ago.

"What does 'runner-up' mean?" she asked.

"Loser," said her dad.

Uncle Ben laughed. "It means second," he told Gloria. "Give us a look."

She gave him the medal.

"I remember this one," he said. "We got beaten, three–two."

"Told you," said her dad. "Loser."

He didn't usually say things—nearly cruel things—like that. But Gloria knew he was joking with Uncle Ben, teasing him. Uncle Ben teased her dad too. They were always doing it to each other.

"Come here, Gloria," said her Uncle Ben.

He held the ribbon so that it became a big triangle, and he put it around Gloria's neck. She felt the weight of the medal on her chest before she looked down and saw it there.

"It's yours now," he said.

"Ah, thanks," said Gloria.

"And Ray," said Uncle Ben. "You too."

Gloria had put all the medals—there were seventeen of

them—in a row, with all the ribbons in a straight line, side by side. Uncle Ben picked one of them. It was another of the runner-up medals. And he did the same thing—he put it around Raymond's neck. He shook Raymond's hand.

"Congratulations," he said.

"Thanks," said Raymond. "Cool."

And Uncle Ben shook Gloria's hand too.

"Congratulations, Gloria."

They laughed.

"I bet it's the only time you'll ever be a runner-up," said Uncle Ben.

CHAPTER 3

They sat under the kitchen table.

They were ready.

Raymond looked at Gloria.

She nodded.

Raymond pressed the little button on the side of his watch.

They'd started. They were going for a new world record. The old one was impressive: one hour and forty-six minutes, and seventeen seconds. It was hard to imagine that they'd ever done it. But they always felt that way at the start, just after they'd crept under the table, after that excitement had worn off and the new excitement had only started. The first part was all thrills, as they'd crawled and slid their way to success. Now success—the new world record—meant doing nothing. Doing absolutely nothing, for absolutely ever. It was agony— and brilliant.

Gloria was able to drift—that was what it felt like. She'd be sitting in exactly the same way, the grown-ups would be chatting and laughing and, after a while, their voices would feel like noise with no real meaning. She wouldn't be listening anymore, she wouldn't be curious. She wasn't asleep or even daydreaming. She was drifting—no story, no pictures or things she had to recognize or understand. She was cloudy and light, lifted by the hum of the voices. Until something would pull her back to where she was, under the table. A louder voice, a sudden laugh, a sneeze, the teapot thumped down on the table above her head. A slippered foot shooting right past her nose. She'd be wide awake, and back. She'd tap Raymond's knee and he'd show her his watch. She was often shocked at how long she'd been away.

But it took a good while for the drifting to start. She had to settle down and get used to being there, and to the way she was sitting. She had to get rid of the giddiness. She had to let it all become normal. To let her heartbeat slow down. To let this—sitting secretly under the table—become a thing that she always did.

But this time it was different. Because they—herself and Raymond—were up close to the mumbling for the first time. Usually the adults would see them, stop mumbling, and smile. But this time the adults didn't know that Raymond and Gloria were near. And they kept mumbling.

There was nothing at first. No one was talking. It was an important part of mumbling— the gaps between the mumbles. Gloria and Raymond had learned that when they'd been listening upstairs in their beds. They'd hear the actual mumbles. They'd try to make out words.

"What are they saying?"

"Don't know—Shhh."

Then they'd stop—the mumbles, the voices, the muffled words. And they'd start again—and stop. And start. And stop again.

"Are they finished, Rayzer?"

"How would I know?"

They'd wait.

Then they'd hear another one. And another.

Now, Raymond and Gloria waited to hear the mumbles properly. This had been the usual adventure until they'd made it, safe and undetected, under the table. Then they knew, separately and together: They wanted to know what was wrong.

Gloria tapped Raymond's knee. He showed her his watch.

Two minutes and seven . . . eight . . . nine seconds.

Gloria knew she wouldn't be drifting tonight.

CHAPTER 4

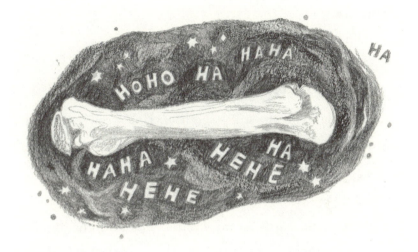

Pat and Una sat at the kitchen table, with Ben and also Una's mother. It had been one of those nights, when more bad news had been delivered.

Una was a bit sick of it. She didn't blame Ben. He was great, and it was lovely having him in the house. He was Pat's little brother, and she'd always called him her little brother-in law.

He was only a teenager when Una and Pat got married. An awkward, lanky, lovely fella—and the worst best man there'd ever been at a wedding. He'd been so nervous he'd forgotten where he'd left the ring the night before.

"Do you have the ring?" the priest had asked.

"What ring?" Ben had answered.

The laughter in the church had been gradual, a ripple that had started at the front and rolled to the back, maybe even out to the street.

"Here," said a woman at the back. "Have mine. I'm getting divorced anyway."

"Did you hear her?"

"Ah, that's priceless."

By the time the wedding was over, everybody loved Ben. Including Una. And she still loved him. He'd grown out of his awkwardness and lankiness and he'd become a very sound man and a good friend.

But it was becoming too much.

No one said anything for a while. The kettle had boiled, and Una's mother was up at the counter, putting the teabags in the pot.

Una didn't know for how much longer this could keep happening. Ben was struggling—so the whole house was struggling. She felt a bit heartless, even thinking like this. But she couldn't help it.

Una's mother put the teapot on the table and sat back down with one of her famous grunts.

Una had to be careful. She didn't want to hurt Ben, or Pat. Or the kids—especially not the kids. Gloria and Raymond adored Ben. And they were right to. He was the best uncle they could possibly have. She'd never have done anything to upset them, or to make them think less of Ben—or her.

And then there was her mother. The children's granny. She'd been living with them for six years now, and it had worked out very well. She had her own little flat. Her own front door, her own little kitchenette, fridge, stove, everything she needed. But she could be a bit tricky, even difficult. Una didn't mind it too much, but her mother got on Pat's nerves. She was very good at it.

Sometimes, at night, he'd lie on the bed, stiff with annoyance.

"She could see I was watching football. She's bloody deaf, not blind."

"She was only making conversation."

"Is that what you call it? 'What are you watching?' 'The football.' 'The what?' 'The football.' 'The what?' She was trying to bully me out of the room, so she could have the telly to herself. She has her own telly."

"She just wants the company."

"It's not company she wants," said Pat. "It's the remote control she wants. That's her evil plan."

"Ah, stop."

"She knew full well it was football."

"She knows nothing about sports," said Una.

It wasn't really an argument. They were having a great time.

"Nothing?" said Pat. "There was a goal, right—while she's asking me what I'm watching. Messi scores this brilliant goal. And do you know what she says? 'He was offside.'"

They were laughing, but it wasn't as easy as that. Una's mother did kind of occupy the place when she felt like it. She had her own key.

"Big mistake, big mistake."

So she came and she went. Or, she came . . . and sometimes she went. So there was a balance—kind of. Pat got Ben, and Una got her mother. Fair and square—sometimes.

Una hated thinking like this. She hated looking at Ben and seeing a problem. She wanted to help. She wished she could do something to make him happier. She could have hugged him, but she already seemed to be hugging him three or four times a day.

Her mother broke the silence.

"That's terrible news," she said. "Isn't it?"

"Yes," said Una. "It is."

Below her, the children were listening. "So," thought Gloria, "this is mumbling."

Una looked across at Ben again. Poor lad.

A few minutes before, he'd told them that he was closing down his painting and decorating business.

"Are you sure about this, Ben?"

Ben shrugged. "A few years ago I stopped answering the phone because I was too busy," he said. "I couldn't keep up. But now . . . the phone never rings."

Raymond saw his Uncle Ben's feet moving. He saw the white paint spots on the boots.

Ben stood up.

"So," he said. "That's that."

Gloria watched her Uncle Ben's feet walk slowly to the kitchen door. She knew by the way he moved that something sad and bad was going on. She wanted to roll out from under the table and run after him. She wasn't sure why she didn't. Maybe because her legs had gone numb. Maybe because she wasn't even sure she was thinking properly. Maybe she'd been doing her drifting.

Then something else happened—it definitely happened. Uncle Ben shut the kitchen door.

Raymond saw it too. He looked at Gloria. She was already looking at him. The kitchen door had never been closed before, not as far as Raymond or Gloria could remember. It was always left open—always. Except when the last adult went up to bed.

They looked at each other. There was no escape. But it was more important than that. The click of the closing door was like a warning sign, or a sound in a film that told you something bad or scary might be coming.

But nothing sudden happened.

The children under the table didn't move.

"Poor Ben," said their mam.

"You'd want to mind that poor lad," said their granny.

Gloria saw her granny's feet move. She was standing up.

"What d'you mean?" said their dad.

"Depression," said Gloria's granny.

Gloria saw her granny's feet turn. Her slippers were two dogs' heads, and the ears bounced on the floor. They were like a pair of mad twins.

Una's mother looked at Pat.

"The black dog of depression has climbed onto that poor fella's back," she said.

Pat and Una both nodded. They knew what she meant. Ben might be suffering from depression. They accepted it, even though it was horrible to hear and they both wanted to cry.

"I'll tell you," said Una's mother. "The whole city seems depressed. So many people you see out there look so unhappy."

They nodded again. She was saying exactly what Pat and Una thought.

"But anyway," said Una's mother. "That's the way of it. I've lived through hard times before, but I've never known anything like this. I've seen the black dog's bad work before, but I've never seen him take over the whole city. I'd be worried about that lad, so I would."

Raymond heard his granny put something on the table—the teapot.

"There's more tea for you," she said.

"Are you not having a cup yourself?" said their mam.

"No, no," said their granny. "I'm off to bed. The politicians can tell their lies, but your bed will never let you down."

Gloria watched her granny's dog slippers as they started to turn again. Gloria saw one heel step on a dog's ear. She saw her granny trip. She heard her granny hit the table.

"Oh God!"

"Are you all right?" said their mam.

Gloria saw their mam push back her chair and start to stand up. They were going to be caught. Their mam was going to see them.

"I'm grand," said their granny. "But I whacked my funny bone."

They heard her groan.

"And it isn't funny at all," she said.

"Are you sure you're all right?"

"I'm grand, I'm grand," said Raymond's granny. "But it makes me think. The funny bone. That's what's happening. The city's funny bone is gone. There's no one laughing anymore."

"You might be right," said Raymond and Gloria's dad.

"I think I am," said their granny. "There's a thought. The black dog of depression stole Dublin's funny bone."

Raymond watched his granny's slippers continue the journey to the kitchen door.

"It's desperate, she said. "What's happening to young Ben and all the others. And no one seems to be willing or able to do anything about it."

She opened the kitchen door.

"Anyway," she said. "I'm off to my little damp granny flat. Night-night."

She walked out and didn't look back. So she didn't see Raymond and Gloria under the table. They heard her walk down the hall. They heard the front door opening, and closing.

Raymond watched his parents' legs and feet. He could tell: They were getting ready to stand up. There was a tiny hole in his dad's sock. He was tempted to lean over and tickle his dad's toe. He really wanted to. But he didn't—he resisted. Something told him his parents wouldn't have liked finding him and Gloria under the table. Not after what they'd been talking—mumbling—about. It wasn't a game, not tonight.

Gloria was looking at her parents' feet too. They'd been getting ready to stand. But they stopped—they paused.

"Her flat isn't damp, is it?" said their mam.

"She's damp," said their dad.

"Ah, stop."

"No," said her dad. "The flat's grand. And I don't know why she said it was damp."

"She was only joking."

"She's hilarious."

"She used to be," said Gloria's mam. "She really was."

Gloria heard her mam sigh.

"Anyway," she said.

Gloria's mam often did that—said "Anyway" and nothing else when she was distracted or a bit low.

Raymond and Gloria watched their parents stand up. They felt closer to each other, even though they hadn't moved. They were trying to make themselves smaller, so their parents wouldn't spot them.

Raymond heard them pick up cups and stuff. He heard their dad.

"Leave them. I'll do them in the morning."

He heard their mam. "Are you sure?"

"Yeah, of course."

"It'll be a pain in the neck in the morning, love," said their mam.

"It'll be a bigger pain now," said their dad.

Gloria heard their mam laugh—or trying to. It came out a bit like a snort.

"Are you worried about Ben?" their mam asked their dad.

"I am, yeah," said their dad. "A bit."

He sighed.

"She's probably right about the depression," he said. "The black dog thing she was talking about. It's a good way of describing depression, isn't it?"

"Yes."

"Black dog," said their dad. "Woof bloody woof."

Gloria watched her mam's feet, then her dad's, his legs, then nearly all of him as he got nearer the door and farther from the table.

He switched off the light. It was suddenly dark—Raymond tried not to gasp.

"We'll keep an eye on him," said their mam.

"I suppose so," said their dad. "But I wish there was more we could do. I just feel so bloody powerless."

He sighed again.

"What a bloody country."

The door clicked shut.

CHAPTER 5

Gloria and Raymond crawled out from under the table.

It wasn't too dark now. There was some light coming in from the kitchen window.

They waited till they heard their parents moving around upstairs. They knew exactly what was happening, as if they were reading a story and the words were written across the ceiling. Their mam went into the bathroom, and their dad went into their bedroom. Their mam turned on the water, their dad closed the bedroom curtains.

Raymond and Gloria waited.

Their mam brushed her teeth, their dad threw his trousers on the floor. Their mam hummed a bit of a song, and their dad did one of his big yawns.

They waited.

Their parents swapped places. Their dad went into the

bathroom. He said something to their mam, and she laughed—but it wasn't a real laugh. Their dad turned on the water, and their mam dropped a shoe on the floor. Their dad crossed the landing, into their bedroom. He closed their bedroom door quietly. They heard their dad lie back on the bed.

Gloria and Raymond looked at each other. And they listened. A few more minutes and they'd hear their dad snore, and the noise of their mam making him move onto his side.

Raymond whispered, "Did you hear what they said?"

"Granny's damp," Gloria whispered back.

"Not that," Raymond whispered. "The other thing. The thing Granny said."

"The Black Dog."

"Yeah," said Raymond. "The Black Dog of Depression took Dublin's funny bone."

They heard the snore—their dad had started. They heard the bed creak, and their dad stopped, as if the snore had been broken in half.

They waited for a few more seconds.

"Yeah," Gloria whispered. "And they're worried about Uncle Ben."

"The Black Dog's been on his back."

"I didn't see him on Uncle Ben's back," Gloria whispered. "Did you, Rayzer?

"No."

It upset them. It was horrible. The Black Dog of Depression definitely wasn't a nice dog, and he'd been climbing onto their uncle's back. They didn't know what the Black Dog did

50

then—licked Uncle Ben with his horrible tongue or whispered horrible things into Uncle Ben's ear. They didn't know. They'd only just heard about the Dog.

They both shivered.

"We have to do something," said Raymond—he whispered.

"What?"

"Get the funny bone back from the Black Dog," Raymond whispered.

"Yeah," Gloria agreed—she whispered too. "It'll cheer up Uncle Ben and make him better again."

"Let's go."

"Hang on," said Gloria. "What's a funny bone?"

"It's the bit of the body that makes you laugh," said Raymond. "You know the way the heart is where your blood goes and the lungs are where your air goes?"

"Yeah."

"Well," Raymond whispered, "the funny bone's where the laughs are stored, before you use them."

"And the Black Dog wants to rob Uncle Ben's funny bone?"

"Not sure," said Raymond. "Think so."

"So Uncle Ben can't laugh."

"Yeah," said Raymond. "Or even smile—without trying really hard."

Gloria nodded. It all made sense. She'd seen her Uncle Ben trying to smile.

"And does Dublin have a funny bone as well?" she whispered.

"Granny said so," said Raymond.

"Ah, well, then," said Gloria.

She trusted her granny, and it still made sense. No one in the city seemed to laugh anymore. No teachers, or any of the other adults she knew.

"Let's go," said Raymond.

"Now, like?"

"Yeah."

"Okay."

Gloria ran to the back door—it was the nearest way out—but Raymond ran to the other door, the one their dad had closed a few minutes before.

Gloria was confused.

"Where are we going, Rayzer?" she whispered.

"Upstairs, to get our clothes on."

"Oh yeah," Gloria whispered. "I forgot."

They were still in their jammies. They'd no shoes or socks on, or anything. She laughed—quietly.

"There's nothing wrong with my funny bone, Rayzer," she whispered.

They crept out into the hall and went quietly back up the stairs. They crept into Raymond's bedroom. They didn't turn on the light. The click of the switch would have been too loud. They took off their pajamas and put on proper clothes. They didn't sit on the bed, so the bedsprings wouldn't creak or squeal. They crept back out to the landing. They went back down the stairs, very carefully over the loose nail in the second-to-last step. They shut the kitchen door again, carefully, quietly.

They sat on the floor and put on their shoes.

"Will we bring our coats?"

"I hate my coat."

"Me too."

Raymond was unlocking the back door, about to step into the night.

The door was open now. The new cold air was all around them.

"Where are we going, Rayzer?" Gloria asked.

"Don't know," said Raymond.

He gulped—it was dark out there.

He took a big breath.

"But we have to find the Black Dog," he said. "And he's not in here. So come on."

They ran out into the back garden. The security light from

O'Leary's house next door went on, with a click and a blast of white light.

"Oh my God!"

"Come on!"

Raymond led the way to the side of the house. It was cold, and there was a smell of old trash bin. O'Leary's security light clicked off.

Raymond stopped.

"I can't see."

He tried to sound casual.

"I might step in something yucky."

"Brilliant," said Gloria, and the word popped open above

them and filled the passage between the houses with gentle yel-low light. They were shocked but not all that surprised.

Brilliant *was the busiest word in Dublin. It was the city's favorite word. Everyone in Dublin said "Brilliant" at least twenty-seven times a day, and more than a million people lived in Dublin. So "Brilliant" was whis-pered, shouted, roared, bawled, screamed, laughed, or just plain said at least twenty-seven million times a day.*

It started first thing in the morning.

"I'm still alive. Brilliant!"

And it went on, all through the day.

"What's for breakfast?"

"The usual."

"Brilliant."

"Oh, look, it's stopped raining."

"Brilliant."

All day.

"Here's the bus."

"Brilliant."

"There's two of them!"

"Double brilliant!"

Wherever people met each other or just walked past, the "Brilliant"s filled the air. Even when there was no one around, a deserted corner or an empty shop, the echoes of the "Brilliant"s bounced and rolled along the walls or ceilings for hours after the people who'd said them had left.

"Brilliant."

"Brilliant."

"Brilliant."

"... brilliant ..."

      "... brilliant ...."

           "......... illia ...."

On the busy streets, in the places where people worked and played, in the schools and playgrounds and the cafes and churches—

"The Lord is my shepherd."

"Ah, that's brilliant."

The offices, the kitchens, the bathrooms, the nurseries, the shopping centers, the libraries—

"Brilliant!"

"Shuushhhhhh!"

"Sorry."

The football fields and tennis courts, the gyms and the swimming pools, the buses, the train stations, the petrol stations and inside the taxis, the hospitals—

"No bones broken, anyway."

"Brilliant."

The pubs and the clubs and the cinemas and theaters, the parks and the waiting rooms, anywhere where there were people, the air was stuffed with "Brilliant"s.

And that was on the quiet days.

"That was a great funeral."

"Brilliant."

It was a great word, really. It burst out of your mouth when you said it.

"How's the soup?"

"Brilliant!"

"Ah, look what you've done to me shirt!"

It was a handy word, very adaptable. It could be used in all sorts of ways.

"The car won't start."

"Well, that's just brilliant."

It made people smile, even when they didn't want to.

"My dog's dying."

"Ah, no. What was his name?"

"Brilliant."

"Ahhh, that's brilliant."

And that was the problem. **Brilliant** was a brilliant word. It lit everything around it. It was hard to see the gloom when the word was constantly bursting all over the city, like a firework display that never ended. But sometimes—only for brief moments, when very few people were talking—the sadness was there to be seen, on the faces, across the shoulders, in the feet. The adults of Dublin were low. They were worried and sometimes angry. They worried about the future. They felt trapped, surrounded by bad news. There was no escape.

But then someone would say, "Brilliant." And the gloom would disappear.

CHAPTER 6

Brilliant," said Gloria, and the word popped open above them and filled the passage with a gentle yellow light that made the trash bins glow.

They knew the light wouldn't last long, so Raymond got going again and Gloria followed him out, past their dad's parked car, out to the street.

Raymond stopped. And so did Gloria.

"Where now, Rayzer?" she said.

They were at the gate. They could go left or right, or straight across the road.

"There are three black dogs on our road," said Raymond.

"Yeah."

"And they all live down this way," said Raymond.

He pointed right.

"Come on."

They ran.

There was something about nighttime. It seemed to make the noise of their shoes much louder. They could hear their steps bouncing off the walls of all the houses. It sounded like there were other people coming up behind them. Gloria looked, but there was no one else.

They ran past three more gates, to Mooney's house. The gate was open. They went—they tiptoed—to the front door. They got down on their knees. Raymond pushed open the letterbox, and, together, they looked through the opening.

They saw two black eyes—and a tongue. The eyes and tongue belonged to Lulu Mooney. The tongue tried to lick their faces through the mail slot. Raymond was very careful letting the flap of the letterbox back down. Lulu was licking his fingers, and he wanted to laugh. He pushed her nose away with a finger and shut the flap. They could hear little happy whimpers from the other side of the door.

"I don't think Lulu's the Black Dog of Depression," said Gloria.

"No," Raymond agreed.

Lulu started barking.

"Run!"

"I am!"

They dashed back to the street. They could hear Mr. Mooney from inside the house.

"Shut up! Or I'll go down there and take that bloody bone from you!"

Gloria stopped running.

"The funny bone!"

"No," said Raymond. "It's just an ordinary bone. It's Lulu's. She's been minding it for years. And it isn't funny. It's disgusting. Come on."

They ran to the next house, the Simpsons'. Gloria stopped again.

"They're not there," she remembered.

Melanie Simpson was in her class at school.

"They've gone away for Saint Patrick's Day," she said.

"Where?"

"Don't know. To the country."

"All of them?"

"Yeah."

"Amigo as well?"

Amigo was the Simpsons' dog.

"S'pose," said Gloria. "They wouldn't leave him on his own. Unless they've trained him to use a can opener."

"Okay," said Raymond.

They hadn't moved while they were talking, and they both thought the same thing—it was better to keep moving. While they ran, they felt like they were hidden, or at least harder to see, if anyone—an adult—was looking out a window.

"Come on."

They ran to the next house, the O'Driscolls'. The O'Driscolls' black dog, Fang, slept in a shed in the back. So this was a tricky mission, harder than just opening a letterbox.

They walked carefully to the side gate. It wasn't locked.

"Sweet."

But it was creaky. The hinges were old and rusty. Raymond held the handle so he could lift the gate a little bit and slowly push it forward.

It worked. The gate made hardly any noise, but the noise it did make was horrible.

He stopped.

They waited.

No lights came on.

Raymond lifted the gate again and pushed till he thought there'd be enough room for them to slide through.

They waited again.

They heard no voices, or feet.

"Come on."

They were able to squeeze through sideways, one at a time. Raymond went first, and they crept down the dark side passage. There was lots of stuff in their way: two bikes, a dead fridge, and smaller things that Raymond couldn't make out.

"Can't see properly."

"Brilliant."

The shed was suddenly bright.

"Now I can."

It stayed bright till they got to the backyard, where it was already bright enough for them to see the things that were in their way: a lawn mower, a wheelbarrow, a fork, an empty bucket. The lawn mower was buried in the grass. The grass was really long, and a bit frightening because it seemed to be making noise and even grabbing at them as they walked through it to the shed.

Gloria spoke very quietly. She wasn't scared—not really —but she wanted to hear a voice, even her own, so the grass would just be grass again and everything would be normal.

"Mam says Mr. O'Driscoll has a bad back," she said, quietly. "And that's why he never cuts the grass."

"Dad says Mr. O'Driscoll's just a waster," said Raymond, quietly.

They were at the shed now. The door was open, but they didn't go in.

"Here, Fang."

They heard Fang's tail thumping the floor of the shed. But he didn't come out.

"Fang?"

His tail thumped the floor again. But his tail was the only part of Fang that moved. They went to the shed and looked in. It was pitch-black. The shed had no window. But they heard Fang—*thump, thump*—and then they could see him. He was lying on his rug, looking at them. It seemed warm in the shed, and the dog smell was nice. So they stepped in.

"Don't shut the door," Raymond whispered.

"There is no door," Gloria whispered back.

They stood there and looked down at Fang.

Fang was older than both of them; he'd always been old. He was a mix of about twenty different breeds, and most of them must have been big. Because Fang was huge.

Gloria remembered why they were there.

"Are you depressed, Fang?" she asked him.

Fang farted.

"Is that depression?" Gloria asked.

"Don't think so," said Raymond. "Or if it is, Dad's really depressed. Here's the test, watch. Fang?"

Fang's tail walloped the floor—and stopped.

"Fang?"

The tail drumming started again.

"See?" said Raymond. "Fang's definitely not the Black Dog of Depression. He's too happy."

He sighed. This job was going to be harder than he'd expected—although he hadn't really expected, or anticipated, anything. There was another black dog on the next street, but Raymond didn't know if there was any point in—

"What are yis doin'?"

The voice came from nowhere.

Gloria screamed, but nothing came out. She could feel the scream in her throat, but it was clinging there, too scared to climb out of her mouth.

Raymond might have screamed too—he wasn't sure. His face was an exploding red ball—that was what it felt like. His heart was in the middle of his head. He couldn't see a thing.

Gloria had never had been afraid of the dark. But it wasn't the dark that had frightened her. It was the voice. A voice with no body.

Her scream finally came out.

". . . ohmygod . . . !"

Then she saw the head.

Raymond saw it too.

An upside-down head.

"Ernie?" said Raymond.

"Wha'?" said Ernie O'Driscoll.

"What are you doing?"

"Hangin' upside down," said Ernie.

"Yeah," said Raymond. "But why?"

His heart was back where it was supposed to be. He could see Ernie O'Driscoll properly now. Ernie was hanging from a wooden beam that went across the shed, just under the roof. His arms were crossed, over his chest. He was hanging by his legs, like a bat.

"Well," said Ernie. "I'm a bit of a vampire, like."

Ernie O'Driscoll's name was well known all along the street. "If you don't do your homework, you'll end up like Ernie O'Driscoll." "If you don't eat your cabbage, you'll end up like Ernie O'Driscoll." Ernie was famous. All the local kids knew about him. But the fact that Ernie was a vampire was red-hot, brand-new news.

"A vampire?" said Gloria.

Ernie nodded once, upside down.

"Since when?" said Raymond.

He saw Ernie nearly every day.

"Last week," said Ernie.

"Oh."

Gloria thought about this.

"Hey, Ernie," she said. "Did you, like, decide to be a vampire?"

"Me ma told me to get a job," Ernie explained. "So there you go."

"Vampire's a job?" said Raymond.

"There's a recession, bud," said Ernie. "We make our own jobs. And it kind o' runs in the family."

Raymond didn't really know what Ernie was talking about.

"Does that mean 'Yeah'?" he asked.

"It does, yeah," said Ernie. "We need young people with vision. That's my motto, like. And I get to stay in bed all day."

Gloria wasn't even a bit scared now.

"This is mad," she said.

"They said that about your man Einstein," said Ernie. "The fella that invented the Xbox."

"I didn't mean you're mad, Ernie," said Gloria.

There was a vampire in the shed who thought she'd just insulted him. But Gloria still wasn't scared—not at all. She thought it was great that she knew a vampire.

"I meant it's mad—cool mad, like," she explained. "Finding you like this. Why are you hanging upside down?"

"Seen it in a fillum," said Ernie. "It's good for the oul' digestion."

"Did you suck someone's blood tonight?"

"An oul' one in Tyrrelstown," said Ernie.

"Deadly," said Gloria. "Did she scream?"

"She didn't even notice," said Ernie. "She was watchin' *EastEnders*. Hang on."

They heard a grunt and the whoosh of Ernie's black cape— and Ernie was standing in front of them.

"Brilliant!"

The shed was suddenly full of light, and they could see Ernie even better.

"You don't look anything like Robert Pattinson, Ernie," said Gloria.

"Ah, well," said Ernie. "He can't have everythin', I suppose."

"Did the light not hurt your eyes there, Ernie?"

He hadn't even blinked.

"Ah, no way," said Ernie. "That's just a story."

"But you really drink blood, don't you?"

"Ah, yeah."

He belched.

"It's heavy goin', but," he said, "but that thing about vampires bein' scared of the sunlight—that was made up to fool people into thinkin' they're safe durin' the day."

Fang thumped his tail again, and that made Raymond remember why they were there.

"We're chasing the Black Dog of Depression, Ernie," he said. "Want to come?"

Ernie thought about it.

"Is he big, is he?"

"Huge," said Gloria. "I'd say so, and anyway."

"Grand," said Ernie. "Dessert, wha'."

He patted his belly, and Gloria laughed.

"What're we waitin' for?" said Ernie.

"Are you coming, Fang?" said Raymond.

Fang thumped his tail and farted.

"There's your answer, bud," said Ernie. "Seeyeh, Fang. Mind the house."

It was dark again, but they heard Fang's tail walloping his rug. They followed Ernie out of the shed. Gloria heard a voice—or she thought she did—behind her.

"Good luck."

She looked back, but there was no one there. Ernie and Raymond were in front of her. So that meant . . . it might have meant that Fang had spoken. Had she just heard a dog speak? It was mad, but, tonight, it wasn't as mad as it should have been. She'd just found out that Ernie was a professional vampire. She'd discovered that a word—*Brilliant!*—could explode into bright and beautiful light.

But it was quite windy. Gloria could hear branches groaning, and, somewhere far off, a door slammed. It was probably just the wind that had made a noise that sounded like "Good luck." But—

"Thanks, Fang," she said over her shoulder, just in case.

Fang didn't answer.

Gloria ran after Raymond and Ernie. Ernie was in the lead, and they followed him out to the front, along the dark side of the house—

"Brilliant!"

And out to the street.

Ernie stopped. He looked up and down the street.

"So," he said. "Where's this black dog?"

"We don't know," said Raymond.

But as he spoke, they saw the Dog. At the end of the street.

Not the Dog exactly—its shadow, and only for a second. It was huge, and it slid against the wall, the side wall of the grocery store, up as high as the upstairs window, as it turned the corner. It made no noise. But it had definitely been the Black Dog.

It was gone. There was no sign of it, or sound. But they'd seen it.

They stood there for a while—excited, scared, uncertain.

Then—

"Come on!"

CHAPTER 7

They ran to the corner as fast as they could, even though they were probably running toward danger.

But the Black Dog had gone. He'd disappeared.

They could look down four streets from here. But there was no sign of the Dog—no sign of anything. It was cold, a kind of moving cold, like a freezing, invisible animal was rubbing against them.

"Well," said Ernie, and he pointed at both streets across from their corner. "He can't have gone down there. We'd have seen him crossin' the road."

The cold crawled around them. There was no sound now from the wind.

"This one," said Raymond, and he pointed left. "Come on."

He started to run, past the front of the grocery store and Hair2Day, the hairdresser's.

"Why that one?" Ernie asked.

"The other one's a culdy-sack," Raymond shouted back.

"Dogs love culdy-sacks," said Ernie.

He was right. Most dogs loved a good cul-de-sac, a trapped street of interesting smells that were going nowhere. But—

"Not this one," said Raymond. "He's definitely going somewhere. Come on."

Gloria was impressed. Raymond sounded like an expert, the Black Dog Hunter. But, really, she didn't want to go any farther. She was frightened—she admitted it to herself. The cold scared her, the way it seemed to move, to creep around her.

But Raymond started running. Gloria thought of her Uncle Ben and the weight of the Black Dog on his back, and she ran after him.

They ran to the next corner.

There was no Black Dog. They could see nothing on the street ahead, no shadow or anything solid. It was very late, very quiet. Very cold.

"Here, Ernie," said Raymond.

He shivered.

"Wha'?" said Ernie.

"Can you not fly?" said Raymond.

"No way," said Ernie.

"I thought vampires could fly."

"Only in the fillums, bud," said Ernie. "We have to get the bus, like everyone else. But look wha' I can do."

He spread out his arms so his cape looked like a huge bat's wings.

"The business, wha'!"

"That's so cool," said Gloria.

Then they felt the cold moving again, around them, like an animal. Rubbing against their legs. It wasn't wind. It was like solid, invisible cold.

"What's happening, Rayzer?"

"Don't know."

The cold seemed to push at them, to make them face the same direction.

And they saw it.

A cloud.

A low, black cloud—it was lower than the house roofs.

Ernie pointed at it. "It's kind o' shaped like a dog."

He was right. The cloud moved away from them. It seemed to become even more dog-shaped as it drifted farther down the street. Two dark wisps looked like its ears.

"It's a bit horrible," said Gloria.

"Yeah," Raymond agreed.

And it was gone again—around a corner.

"Come on!"

Ernie was fastest. He ran ahead, down the new street, and Raymond and Gloria followed. He waited for them at every corner, and at every corner they were quickly cold. The corner was a cold hint, something the Black Dog seemed to be leaving behind, telling them which way to run.

Raymond wondered if they were really chasing the Dog or if the Dog was leading them somewhere. It didn't matter, he decided—he didn't think too much about it. Because they still had to catch the Dog.

They could see the Dog ahead, then gone, then back. He was playing with them, maybe—although it wasn't funny or anything like funny.

They kept running. But they were tiring.

"Look!" said Gloria, and she pointed.

They were running past Uncle Ben's empty house. The timing was perfect, a reminder of why they were out in the cold. They could see the neighbors' dogs, Chester and Sadie, at their windows. They were barking, but Gloria could hardly hear them.

"That's amazing," she said as she ran.

"What?"

"Sadie's barking," said Gloria.

"What about it?" said Raymond.

"It sounded like, 'Go get him, girl!'"

"Didn't hear it," said Raymond.

They ran. They stayed warmer that way and running seemed to be the right way to measure their love for Uncle Ben. They wanted to hear their breath, and their feet stamping the ground. They wanted to feel their lungs working, and their hearts.

"Where are we, Rayzer?" asked Gloria, after a while.

"Don't know," said Raymond.

They'd run out of the place they knew, the area they would have called home. None of the buildings around them were familiar.

"Look!"

Raymond had just seen it—the Dog.

"Oh my God!"

It was moving, just a shadow, right under a bunch of small trees, in front of a huge, long building.

They knew the building. They'd been here before, loads of times. They were at the Liffey Valley Shopping Centre.

The Dog was a shadow moving through other shadows. A darker shadow, sliding, rolling slowly. Gloria could feel her heart pumping.

"Come on," said Raymond.

"There's not much blood in a shadow," said Ernie, and he sounded disappointed.

Gloria tried to laugh. But she couldn't. Her mouth was too dry.

There were no cars or people—it was very late. It was just Raymond, Gloria, Ernie. And the shadow. Raymond ran straight at it.

He couldn't believe he was doing this, running at his biggest fear, charging straight into darkness. "But," he thought, "it's only a shadow." He knew that shadows were easily explained. They were made of light and shade. So he wasn't just surprised when his hands touched something solid.

He was terrified.

"Aaah!"

"What's the story?" said Ernie.

"I felt it!"

"Felt what, Rayzer?" said Gloria.

"The Dog," said Raymond. "The fur."

"But there's nothing here," said Gloria. "It's gone."

She was right—but she wasn't. There was no dog near them, or in among the trees. But there *was* something.

The cold.

It seemed to be right over them now, a dark, icy cloud. Or a freezing, silent animal leaning over them.

"Ah, here," said Ernie. "It's only a cloud."

Now Gloria laughed.

"Brilliant!"

And the cloud—the weird patch of extra darkness—moved away.

"It's not even dog-shaped," said Gloria.

They weren't sure now if it was even there.

"It was definitely fur," said Raymond.

Gloria believed him. They were looking up at the sky, searching for the cloud, trying to make it out in the darkness.

"Poor Rayzer," she said. "It must have been disgusting, was it?"

"A bit," said Raymond.

"Here," said Ernie. "Why are we doin' this, and anyway?"

"For Uncle Ben," said Gloria. "Me and Rayzer's uncle. He's depressed."

"And the Black Dog has stolen Dublin's funny bone," Raymond told Ernie.

"And Uncle Ben will get better if we can get the funny bone back," said Gloria.

"Says who?" said Ernie.

"Our granny," said Gloria.

"Ah, well, then," said Ernie. "Fair enough."

"Do you know our granny, Ernie?"

"No," said Ernie. "But I always feel brainier after I've drunk a granny's blood."

"Really?"

"On the level."

"Deadly," said Gloria. "But you're to promise not to drink our granny's blood, Ernie. She'd freak out, she would. Ernie?"

"Wha'?"

"Promise."

"Okay," said Ernie. "I promise. But it's against me principles."

"That's it there," said Raymond, pointing down the street, and up. "Look."

The cloud was back—it was definitely there.

"Is it only a cloud, Rayzer?"

Gloria hoped it was, just a cloud behaving strangely. But that made her feel bad because she knew she was supposed to hope it was the Dog. But this—the cloud, the shape, whatever it was—was more frightening than a solid dog, even a huge one, would have been.

"Rayzer?" she said. "Is it only a cloud?"

"I heard you the first time," said Raymond.

They stood still, looking.

"Well, is it?" Gloria.

"Don't know," said Raymond. "Don't think so."

"Is it a mirage?"

"Wrong time of day, honey," said Ernie. "You only see mirages in the daytime, I think."

"It has to be hot for a mirage," said Raymond.

"Then it's definitely not a mirage," said Ernie. "I'm freezin'."

"Maybe it's nothing," said Gloria.

She knew what she was doing, what they were doing. They were filling the air around them with their voices, protecting

78

themselves against the silence. The cloud was less scary while they talked.

"Maybe it's just something we think we can see," she said.

But, as Gloria spoke, they watched the cloud sink to the street, and it stopped being something they thought they'd seen and became something solid and real that they could definitely see. The cloud had black streaks that looked like legs. They touched the ground.

"The Dog!"

"Oh my God!"

A big black dog. A big, ordinary dog—they could even hear his paws smack the ground as he ran away.

What they'd just seen, a strange cloud changing into a black dog, was frightening, nothing close to anything Gloria and Raymond had ever seen before. But the result of the change was far less terrifying. The Black Dog was scary—but he was still just a dog.

"Come on!"

They ran down a road that was a steep hill, where cars leaving the shopping center rolled onto the main road, back to Dublin or away in the other direction, to the country. There were no cars or trucks now, though—it was too late. They had to slow down because the slope was making them go too fast. Their chests and heads were going ahead of their legs, and they'd have toppled over. They could see the Dog clearly under the streetlights. They could see his coat gleaming, like he was healthy and well looked after.

Gloria knew which way they were going. She knew she lived in Dublin West and that the rest of Dublin was to the east. She'd learned that in school. She'd followed the main road, the N4, on the map with her finger, from where she lived to the city center. She'd loved it, that you could see a real place, a place as big as Dublin, on a page that fit into a schoolbook. They were running east now, toward the city—or "town," as their parents always called it. Farther east, there was Dublin Bay and the sea. The River Liffey flowed east too. It was beside them, somewhere near, to their left—although Gloria couldn't see or hear it. They wouldn't see the river till they got to town, but Gloria didn't know if they'd have to go that far before they caught up with the Black Dog. She didn't know—she just ran.

Raymond was the first to run off the sloping road and onto the N4. "This is great," he thought. "I'm doing something." He was chasing the Dog. He wasn't sure why, exactly. It wasn't as clear as that. He just knew that the Dog had the funny bone. He couldn't see the bone sticking out of the Dog's mouth, and he hadn't seen it earlier, when the Dog had climbed out of the cloud.

But, for now, that didn't matter. He was chasing the Dog. He was saving his Uncle Ben.

There were cars here, all going in the same direction as Gloria, Raymond, and Ernie. They were running on the hard shoulder—that was what the side of the road was called. The car lights lit the Dog ahead of them. They hadn't been running for long, so Gloria had plenty of breath for talking.

"Why's it called the hard shoulder?"

She asked Ernie, because he was the oldest.

"Haven't a clue," said Ernie. "'Cos it's hard, I suppose."

"Maybe it's called that because you'd break your shoulder if you fell on it."

"Nice one," said Ernie.

Raymond was well ahead of them now.

"Hurry up!" he shouted back.

"What's his problem?" said Ernie.

"He's right," said Gloria. "Come on."

Raymond could hear his sister and Ernie catching up. He didn't want to be by himself when he caught up with the Dog. But he wasn't scared—not really.

"Sorry, Rayzer."

It was Gloria beside him, puffing from the effort. Ernie was beside him too. But he wasn't moving his arms or feet. He was standing straight, like a statue, but rolling along beside them.

"Are they skates?" Raymond asked, and he pointed at Ernie's shiny shoes.

"Not at all," said Ernie. "I just keep forgettin' I can do this."

"Do what, Ernie?"

"Dunno," said Ernie. "I suppose you'd call it glidin'."

"Deadly."

"Yeah," said Ernie. "One of the perks of the job."

"Can you carry me?"

"I can, yeah," said Ernie. "But I won't."

They stopped talking then. They weren't tired yet—not nearly—but talking took too much breath and energy. And the passing traffic was hard work too. The cars and trucks cut through the air and sent invisible waves that shoved right against them and nearly pushed them off the hard shoulder. Paper flew around them, and empty plastic bottles bounced between their feet. But it didn't stop or slow them down.

They didn't speak. They kept going and they kept up with the Dog. Small stones flew from under car wheels and shot past, low, sometimes whacking their shoes and trouser legs. But it was good, Raymond and Gloria decided, although they didn't say it to each other. The stones, the bottles, and the trucks— they were all trying to slow them down, to stop them. But they couldn't, because Gloria and Raymond wouldn't let them. They were fighting, and winning. A sharp little stone nipped Gloria's ankle, but she didn't care. She was doing this for her Uncle Ben. A stinging ankle didn't matter.

Sometimes they seemed to be catching up, even though they were getting a bit tired now and Ernie had forgotten that he could glide. His shiny vampire shoes were a bit big for him and they were slapping the road as he ran. Sometimes the Dog seemed to be getting away, but they could still hear him—his breath and his paws on the road—just ahead.

Gloria had a thought.

"Is he letting us chase him?"

Raymond had been thinking the same thing.

"Don't know," he said. "Maybe."

"But why?"

"Don't know."

"It might be a trap," said Ernie.

"Yeah," said Raymond. "But what kind?"

"The usual," said Ernie.

"What's that?"

"One you get caught in."

But they kept running. Trap or no trap, they still had to catch the Black Dog.

They could see the Phoenix Park ahead, and the shape of the trees. They were surprised, and pleased. It usually took ages to get this far in their dad's car. But there it was, just ahead. The trees were a blacker shape against the black of the night sky.

"What's that noise?"

They could hear other feet, other shoes hitting the ground, behind and nearly beside them—a few at first, then more. Gloria slowed down, so she could look.

"What's going on, Rayzer?"

They began to see the other kids. They came running out of the dark. There were two of them, then four, eight—more.

Boys and girls, brothers and sisters, like Gloria and Raymond, and others by themselves. No grown-ups. All kids—children.

All of them were running.

And Gloria knew: They were all chasing the Black Dog.

ut the Dog was gone.

"Where is he?"

They could still hear his paws slapping the ground, but they couldn't see him.

"Where is he, Rayzer?"

Raymond didn't know.

It was a shock—and frightening.

They all slowed down. They couldn't see anything, just the road and the traffic. There was nothing to follow. Running had stopped making sense.

"I don't like this," said Gloria.

Raymond agreed. "Yeah."

They'd been in control, following the Dog, trying to catch him. But they weren't in control anymore.

The Dog was.

They were near town now, on the stretch of road that led

down to Heuston Station and the River Liffey. They all stood there looking at one another. It was hard to tell how many kids there were. Gloria was counting them. There were more than twenty, and she thought there were more behind the ones she could see.

Gloria whispered to Raymond again.

"Do they all know Uncle Ben?" she asked.

"No," said Raymond. "No way. We'd know them if they did."

He looked worried.

"Wouldn't we?"

"I know!" said Gloria. "They all have uncles of their own."

"Yeah," said Raymond. "That makes sense."

Then they felt it—the cold. It was the cold they'd felt earlier, just after they'd left their house and recruited Ernie. It was the same sliding cold, the freezing, invisible animal. But it was even colder now, and harder. Gloria could feel it pushing against her legs. Everyone felt it. The cold was telling them which way to look, which way to go— pushing them.

They all started to run, as if they were obeying an order. They turned left, off the main road, and went over a bridge. They were crossing the Liffey, but they didn't stop to look. Phoenix Park was right in front of them, like a cliff of huge trees rising out of the ground as they got nearer. There was another road running beside the park, and a junction. They could go left or right.

They all slowed down. They hesitated.

"Which way now?"

"Where's the Dog gone?"

Gloria heard a voice: "Left."

They started to run again. They all turned left, all obeying the voice. Gloria had definitely heard it. She was sure it had been a woman's voice, the kind of voice a nice teacher would have had.

But there was no woman there. She looked back as she ran, but all she saw was a cat, a black one. It was sitting on a pillar, and it was looking at Gloria.

But it was only a cat.

She kept going.

They were running through the gate, into Phoenix Park. Their parents would have gone mad if they'd seen Raymond and Gloria going into the park in the middle of the night. They'd have been grounded for weeks, or for months, forever. And again Gloria wondered.

"Why is the Dog letting us chase him?"

No one answered.

They kept running, up a steep path. It was darker now because there were trees on both sides of them, blocking the moon, and they were running away from the streetlights.

Raymond hated it. He hated the fact that he was running straight into darkness, with even more darkness behind it, miles of darkness—Phoenix Park was one of the biggest parks in Europe. He was running away from the lights and traffic sounds and the other sounds of the city. He didn't want to shout "Brilliant." He didn't want to be the first to do it.

He was one of the oldest kids there. He'd had a quick look around and nearly all of the others looked smaller than him. He didn't want them to know he was afraid of the dark. They'd laugh at him, and run past him, leave him alone at the edge of the darkness. He couldn't let them know. But he knew why he was there. He recited it quietly as he breathed in and out. "Uncle Ben . . . Uncle Ben . . . Uncle Ben." He ran into the dark.

They had to be careful because the ground was rough and it was hard to see it clearly.

"Why are you chasing the Black Dog?" Gloria asked the girl who was running beside her.

"My mam," said the girl.

"Oh," said Gloria. "Is she depressed?"

"Yeah," said the girl. "She's down in the dumps, like. My auntie said something about getting the Black Dog off her back. And then I seen him."

"Me too," said a boy. "My da stays in bed all day since his job got shut down."

The boy was panting. They were still running along the path, up a hill.

"The Black Dog blocks the bedroom door," said the boy.

"Have you seen him?" Gloria asked.

"My da?"

"The Black Dog."

"No," said the boy. "But my da has."

"I'm Gloria, by the way," said Gloria.

"Paddy," said the boy.

"I'm Suzie," said the girl.

They kept puffing up the hill.

"Where's the Dog now, but?" Gloria asked.

There was still no sign of him. They couldn't hear him, either. All they could hear was the wind in the trees and their own breath.

They all stopped running. They listened.

Then they felt it again, the rush of cold wind. It went right past them, up close. Then it came back, on the other side. It pushed them—it seemed to—off the path, onto the high grass.

Then they could see it, the darker shape in the darkness, going into the trees. They heard paws going through the grass—and panting. The panting that only dogs make. And they could see the Dog. He barked—he yapped—just before he disappeared into the extra darkness of the trees. He barked like a normal dog, like a dog that liked to play and loved being chased.

"Come on!" Raymond shouted.

They started to run at the trees. Then they heard a voice.

"Be careful!"

"Oh my God! Who said that?"

"None of us," said Raymond. "It was an old man's voice. Come on!"

He noticed the owl as it flew over their heads. He'd never seen one before, except on TV. But he didn't stop to look. He kept running. He made sure he was at the front.

The owl landed on a branch high above the children. He settled beside another owl.

"They wouldn't listen to me," he said.

"That's young people for you," said the other owl. "You were like that yourself once."

"Ah, lay off," said the first owl.

"Anyway," said the second owl. "They have to work this out for themselves."

"You're right," said the first. "But I'm worried."

"So am I," said the second. "But we have to trust them."

"I know," said the first.

He sighed.

"I know."

The kids were in among the trees. And lost. They were stepping among tangled things, trying not to trip. They weren't really a group anymore, and, one by one, they began to realize it. They looked left and right but saw no one. They could hear panting and grunts in front and behind them. But in the pitch dark, being grabbed at by twigs and tripped by things on the ground they didn't want to see and sometimes seemed to scurry, they all felt very alone.

Every careful step she took, Gloria expected to be tripped by a tree stump or brambles or—the word popped into her head—*undergrowth*. She was starting to feel trapped. She looked around but she couldn't see anyone.

"Hello?"

Raymond thought he was being grabbed by branches. They held onto his clothes and wouldn't let go. He wanted to shout, to answer Gloria, but he couldn't.

Paddy knew there were no snakes in Ireland. He'd always known that, since even before he'd started going to school. He'd even been named after the saint who'd got rid of all the snakes.

Saint Patrick had rounded up the snakes and he'd kind of bullied them, his da had told Paddy, right into the sea. But then his teacher, Mad Miss Delaney, had told them about people who'd bought snakes—"during the boom," she'd said. They'd got them as pets and then they'd released them into the "wild" because they couldn't afford to feed them anymore. Only, there was no real "wild" in Ireland, Mad Miss Delaney had said, no desert or jungle for a snake to get lost in. "And that's the problem," she'd said. "There are snakes in Ireland. There are lots of snakes in Ireland. Whole families of them. Even in the Phoenix Park."

Paddy was terrified. But he kept going. He was doing this, walking over the snakes, for his da. He wanted his da back—the happy man Paddy had known all his life. Until a year ago, when his da came home from work and told them all—Paddy and his little brothers, and his ma—that there was no more work, that the building site was closed, the gate was chained and locked, and his tools were locked inside. He'd been okay at first—his da. It had actually been good, because his da was at home more of the time. He was a better cook than his ma; even she admitted it. And he'd sometimes meet Paddy and his brothers outside the school, with a ball under his arm, and they'd play football in the park for an hour before they'd walk home. But then the Black Dog arrived. Paddy didn't see him, but he knew something was wrong. His da was staying in bed in the mornings, and he was getting skinny and old looking. His ma looked sad and worried. He heard the woman next door, Mrs. Brennan, say something

about a black dog bringing depression into the house, and his ma said it was like the Black Dog was stretched out in front of the bedroom door, blocking it, and stopping his da from getting out and living again. Then Paddy saw the Dog—last night.

He was stuck. He couldn't move. There was something strong pulling the back of his jacket, and his feet were up against something big that he couldn't see. Paddy could feel it push against his knees, like it was trying to trip him. He was afraid it would move and become one of those huge snakes, a python—a boa constrictor. They ate things whole. They choked them first, then swallowed them—animals, even big ones, birds. People. Paddy couldn't move. He couldn't shout—his throat was too dry and tight.

Suzie was lost. Really lost. She could see nothing now. Absolutely nothing. It was like being locked in a cupboard. But cupboards were warm and always stayed the same shape. This was different. This was frightening.

But she kept going. She took another step. She felt a breath at her face. It stank. But she didn't scream. She stayed calm— she tried to. She thought of her mam, before the Dog had got into the house. That was what had happened, her Auntie Nuala had told her. "Depression," her auntie had said, "is like a big heavy black dog on your back." Her auntie showed her. "Right across your shoulders and neck, even your head." But Suzie couldn't see the Dog. It annoyed her and upset her. She wanted to push the Dog out of the house. But it was invisible; she couldn't see it near her mam. Until last night.

She couldn't move. Her foot was caught in something.

She called out.

"Here!"

But no one answered.

The others were lost or stuck, surrounded by things that they couldn't see. Some of them were so frightened and anxious, they couldn't remember why they were there. It was like waking up in a bad dream, instead of escaping from it. All of them, Gloria and Raymond too—even Ernie—had had this dream before, being trapped in a dark, cold jungle. But this wasn't a dream, and they weren't going to wake up. Because they were already awake.

The Dog howled now, and Gloria's question, "Why is he letting us chase him?" seemed to answer itself.

"It's a trap," said Gloria.

But no one heard her.

Then she heard the voice.

"I'm not going to bite you," said the voice.

It was the Dog. Gloria was sure of it, even though she couldn't see him.

"No," said the voice, the Dog. "You're not worth biting."

It was a horrible voice. It was low and sneering, and kind of wet. Gloria could feel it on her skin, her face and neck. She tried to rub it off.

"You're useless."

The voice came with a stink.

"That's right," said the voice. "That's how useless you are. That's what happens to everything around you. It all starts to rot."

Gloria wanted to cry. She felt the Dog's fur now, against her face. It was rough, and wet.

"Useless," he whispered.

He was right up beside her. He was sliding, swimming around her. She couldn't hear the others now at all. It was quiet, silent, as if the Dog was whispering the same thing privately to all of them. She still couldn't see him.

But he was definitely there. She wasn't asleep.

"You're no good to anyone," he said.

Gloria knew that wasn't true. But she *felt* like it was true. She was going to lie down on the cold ground.

"Good idea," said the Dog.

She'd lie down and escape, close her eyes and drift away, home. She just had to lie down. She just had to close her eyes. She just had to forget.

"Excellent idea," the Dog sneered.

She was bending down toward the ground.

"That's right."

But then she had a different idea.

"Brilliant."

She whispered it, and it produced a tiny, whispered light that was hardly there.

She heard a groan.

She said it again.

"Brilliant."

Louder. The groan was farther away this time. The Dog was moving, slouching away. The stink was gone, and she could see the Dog in the new light. He was just a big dog, running away. From Gloria. And she knew the Dog was a liar. She wasn't useless.

"Brilliant!" she shouted. "Rayzer!"

"Here."

"Shout *Brilliant!*"

"Brilliant!"

The trees were lovely. Then it was dark again.

"Hey, Ernie!" Gloria roared.

". . . Wha'?"

Ernie sounded sad and three-quarters asleep.

"Shout *Brilliant!*"

". . . Why, like?"

"Just do it!"

". . . Okay. Brilliant, brilliant, bleedin' brilliant!"

The trees were lit and gorgeous, like in a film. Gloria could see the other kids now. Some of them were getting up off the ground. They all looked like they'd been asleep and stuck in a horrible nightmare that was still holding on to them.

"Everyone shout!" said Gloria. "Brilliant! Come on!"

"Brilliant," said Paddy.

It felt good, hearing his own voice, knowing he was awake again, and safe.

Suzie yelled it, and laughed.

Raymond laughed too. He lifted his arms and thumped the air above him—"Yesss!"

They all walked side by side through the sparkling trees. They could hear the Dog charging away from their voices. They could hear his paws. And they could see him now too, through the trees.

The trees stopped being so thick and close together. They could see the sky, clouds rolling above them.

They came out of the trees. Gloria felt like she'd been in there, walking through the forest, for days. They all felt that way. They looked at one another, like people who hadn't met in ages.

They kept walking, till they were well clear of the trees and the damp cold that seemed to cling to them.

Then they stopped and gathered together.

"Is everyone here?" asked Raymond.

Most of them, the older ones, looked around.

"How can we tell?," asked Paddy.

It was a good question. It wasn't a school outing or a group of friends on an adventure. They'd never met until just before they'd run into the park. Gloria looked around. She knew her brother, and Ernie. She knew Paddy's name, and Suzie's. She smiled at Suzie. But she knew no one else. So Paddy's question, "How can we tell?," was a good one, and a bit horrible. They couldn't tell if anyone was missing.

"What'll we do, Rayzer?" Gloria asked.

"We'll count who's here," said Raymond.

"Listen up," he said to everybody. "Find out the name of whoever's beside you, and the next time we stop, make sure you can see them."

"Good idea," said Paddy.

They stood still while Raymond quickly counted. They watched through the darkness as the Black Dog ran toward the zoo. They asked one another their names—

"James."

"Chantelle."

"Suzie."

"Cormac."

"Ailish"

"Glenn"

"Mark."

"Paula."

"Conor."

There were four Conors, and two Aislings, a Precious, a Sunday, three Hollys, and a Boris.

Raymond was finished.

"Forty-seven," he said. "Everyone remember."

"Forty-seven," said Suzie.

"Forty-seven," said Boris.

The Black Dog was nearly at the zoo wall.

"Is he getting bigger?"

"Think so . . . Don't know . . . Maybe."

"Come on!"

"Hang on," said Gloria. "Should we not check if there's anyone still, like, asleep in the trees?"

No one wanted to go back in there. But no one wanted to say no.

Then they heard a voice.

"It's fine."

They couldn't see anyone, but the voice seemed to be coming from behind them, high up in the trees.

"You left no one behind."

The voice was calm, and nice—a granddad's voice.

"Come on!"

They ran.

"There they go," said the owl to his friend, the second owl.

"They listened to you that time," said the second owl.

"Yes," said the first owl.

"Do you think they'll make it?" the second owl asked.

"Well," said the first owl. "They've got this far."

"I'm impressed."

"Me too."

"So, who knows?" said the first owl. "They might just do it."

"We're in trouble if they don't."

"That's true," said the first owl. "But look at them down there. They're brave."

"Yes," said the second owl. "They are."

CHAPTER 9

They watched the Black Dog jump over the wall of the zoo. He seemed to be even bigger.

"Can we not just, like, go home?" asked the boy called Cormac.

"No," said Raymond. "We have to stop him."

"Yeah," said Gloria—she was puffing a bit. "And now we know how to do it."

"How?"

"With *Brilliant*."

"Oh yeah."

They were running into danger—they were running after it, chasing it. They all knew that. But running was easier than staying still, and no one wanted to be left behind—alone.

"Look it!" Ernie shouted.

"Deadly."

There were more kids running toward them, from the other side of the park.

"Breakfast," said Ernie.

"Shut up, Ernie," said Gloria.

"Only messin'," said Ernie. "Rice Krispies'll do for me."

"Come on!"

They all kept running toward the zoo.

But the zoo was shut. It was still dark, so everything was locked up and there was no one behind the glass where you paid to get in.

The walls were very high.

"He jumped over that," said Chantelle. "I seen him."

"All dogs can jump," said Sunday.

"It's too high to climb over," said Gloria. "What'll we do?"

Ernie shrugged. "Don't know."

"The zoo will be open in a couple of hours," said one of the Conors.

"We can wait," the boy called Cormac suggested.

"No . . . way," said a new girl, Alice.

She'd just arrived, and she was puffing a bit. She hadn't even stopped running when she spoke.

"There's no . . . way I'm . . . waiting."

"Yeah," said another kid, then another.

"We have to get the Dog, remember."

"How, but?"

It was harder to stay brave when they were just standing there, and it was cold and dark. The bad dream with the Dog was still floating around their heads, whispering in their ears—"Useless!"

They kept staring at the wall. It seemed to be growing even higher.

But then Raymond spoke.

"Ernie."

"Wha'?" said Ernie.

"Hold me," said Raymond.

"Wha'?" said Ernie. "No way."

"Go on," said Raymond. "I'll climb on your shoulders."

"No, you won't," said Ernie.

"Listen," said Raymond. "I go on your shoulders—"

Paddy was about to object. He wanted to be in on the plan as well. But then he heard Raymond.

"And Paddy can get up on my shoulders and all the others can climb up us onto the wall."

"Cool."

"Ah, great," said Ernie. "And everyone here gets to stand on my head with their mucky feet."

"Go on, Ernie," said Gloria. "It's the only way."

She loved the idea. She couldn't wait to see it happening.

"No," said Ernie. "I'm a vampire, not a ladder."

"Ah, Ernie."

"Can I bite a few ankles on their way past me fangs?"

"No way, Ernie."

Ernie sighed. "Not fair."

He stood with his back to the zoo wall and bent one of his knees, so Raymond could start climbing.

He held out his hands.

"Come to Ernie."

106

They all watched as Raymond climbed from Ernie's knee, to his hip, to his shoulders. Raymond rested his back against the wall. Then they watched as Paddy climbed from Ernie's knee, to his hip, to his head—

"Ouch!"

"Sorry."

—to his shoulders, to Raymond's knee, hip, and shoulders.

Gloria and Suzie and the new girl helped the little kids climb up Ernie, to Raymond's waiting hands.

Gloria nudged the new girl, Alice.

"That's my brother," she said, proudly.

"Who?" said Alice. "The vampire fella?"

"No way," said Gloria. "The other one. Rayzer."

"Is he in charge?" asked a new boy, Damien.

"Yeah," said Gloria. "Kind of."

Some of the others nodded. None of them knew Raymond, but they liked him. They liked being near him. He made them feel braver, and a bit safer.

"Who's next?"

"Me!"

"No, me!"

Ernie grabbed the smallest kid, a boy.

"Come here, Snack."

"Ernie," Gloria said, warning him.

"Only messin'," said Ernie, and he held the boy up till Raymond grabbed him and passed him up to Paddy. The smallest kid was laughing. The others watched him climb up Paddy, holding on to Paddy's jeans and hoodie. He got on to the wall and sat down. They laughed, and forgot they were frightened.

"Me next!"

They were all on the wall now, in less than three minutes. Gloria was the last to be delivered.

"Here we go," said Ernie, and he held her gently under her arms.

Her feet left the ground.

"Thanks, Ernie."

"No sweat," said Ernie.

She climbed past Ernie—"Seeyeh, Ernie"—past Raymond —"Seeyeh, Rayzer"—and on, up to Paddy. She could see over the wall now, all the trees and the lake and the African section, way at the back of the zoo. The other kids made space for her and she sat down.

There was no one left except the three boys who'd been the ladder. Paddy lifted one of his legs from Raymond's shoulder. He looked like he was going to jump but he turned and grabbed the top of the wall. Damien and Alice helped him up.

That left Raymond and Ernie.

Paddy lay on his stomach on the top of the wall.

"Hold my legs," he said to Damien and Alice.

Raymond did what Paddy had done. He stepped off Ernie, and turned. He held up his hands, and Paddy grabbed them. Then Raymond climbed the rest of the way, holding on to Paddy's arm.

Ernie was the only one left.

"How will you get up, Ernie?" Gloria called down.

"Haven't a clue," said Ernie.

They heard a loud squawk and saw a big seagull fly down and land on top of a trash bin near the wall, then fly—nearly jump— off the bin, up over the wall, right over their heads.

"Hey, Ernie—"

"I know," said Ernie. "I'll follow the seagull. Nothin' to it."

They watched as Ernie walked away, back toward the trees. Gloria began to think that he was going home, when he turned and started to glide—fast. He was heading straight for the bin. Just before he got to it, he stopped gliding and started to run properly—fast—really fast. Then he jumped.

They gasped and cheered. Ernie's cape spread out behind him. It looked like he was really flying as he landed on top of the bin and jumped—bent his legs and pushed—at the wall.

"Uh-oh!"

He went right over it.

Gloria couldn't watch—but she did, she had to. She watched Ernie, in midair, as he reached back and grabbed the bottom corners of his cape with both hands and held them up.

Ernie's cape had become a parachute, and Ernie floated to the ground, inside the zoo.

He landed, fell, stood up, and shook his cape.

"Nothin' to it," he said.

The kids on the wall cheered and clapped. It was the coolest thing most of them had ever seen.

Ernie stood with his back to the wall, and Raymond lowered himself on his shoulders.

"Wipe your feet," said Ernie.

Paddy stood on Raymond shoulders, facing the wall, and the kids climbed and crawled down his back, to Raymond, to Ernie, to the ground. They were all less frightened now—the bigger kids too—inside the zoo.

Gloria landed, then Paddy, then Raymond.

They were ready to go.

But that was the new problem. Where had the Dog gone?

"Ernie," said Raymond.

"Wha' now?"

"Can you see the Dog?"

"No."

"Not from here, Ernie," said Gloria, and she pointed at the nearest bin. "From up there."

"Gotcha," said Ernie, and he started to glide across to it.

"That's so cool," said Precious.

They all watched as Ernie jumped and landed on the bin.

"See anything, Ernie?"

"Over there," said Ernie. "The big things. The what're-they-called? The elephants."

He pointed ahead, a bit to the right.

"They're goin' a bit mad," said Ernie.

"Come on!" said Raymond.

"Come on!" said Damien, who didn't see why he should do everything Raymond told him to.

"Come on!" said Alice, who didn't see why she had to do everything two skinny boys told her to.

"Come on!" said Paddy, who thought Alice was lovely.

They all ran together. They felt bigger together, stronger, and their feet made big noise on the path. There were no clouds now; the sky was clear. So they could see where they were running.

They ran past the meerkats.

"Go get him, kiddos!"

"Who said that?" Gloria asked Suzie.

"Don't know," said Suzie.

They kept running.

Damien wanted to go faster, to pass Raymond and be at the front. And Raymond wanted to pass Damien. But they had to let the other kids stay up with them, especially the little ones. There weren't sure why, but they knew they needed as many kids as possible to catch the Dog and capture the funny bone. But it made their legs sore, having to run slowly.

Raymond decided not to hate Damien and, immediately, running slowly became easier.

"What's your name?" he asked.

"Damien."

"Mine's Ray."

The kids dashed past the lemurs and spider monkeys.

"I'm glad I'm not paying for this," said Paddy. "It'd be a terrible waste of money."

Alice laughed, and Paddy was delighted. He was thrilled and all-powerful. He was going to punch the Dog so hard, he'd send him into the middle of next week. Or last week—he wasn't sure which.

Alice was happy too. She thought Paddy was massive, and she'd decided in her head that they were on their first date—and *her* very first date.

"Oh, look," she said. "The snake house."

"Not interested," said Paddy.

There was no way he was going to look at any snakes.

But he felt terrible, like a coward. He could imagine punching the Black Dog in the nose, but he couldn't look at a snake, or a building that had a snake in it.

They ran past the lake and the pink flamingos standing beside it. But they didn't stop to look.

"This is a zoo—hellohhhoh?"

"Who said that?"

"Don't know."

Gloria was running with Ernie.

"Is it good being a werewolf, Ernie?"

"Couldn't tell yeh," said Ernie. "I'm a vampire."

"Oh yeah. Is it any good?"

"It's all righ'," said Ernie. "It's a bit borin'."

"You like drinking blood, though, don't you?"

"I'll tell yeh one thing," said Ernie. "It beats orange juice."

"I hate orange juice."

"You're nearly a vampire yourself, so."

"Deadly."

Gloria was feeling almost happy. The woods and the evil whispers were far behind her. They had the Dog on the run, and she knew they'd be able to beat him.

They were off the main path, and they were running along a forest trail, getting nearer and nearer to the elephants. They couldn't see as much now because the trail was bendy and the trees were close, leaning over, like a green and brown roof above them.

Paddy was still running beside Alice. He took a deep breath and spoke before he could change his mind. "It would be cool to come back and see the zoo properly. Together, like, another time. Wouldn't it?"

"No," said Alice.

All the breath left Paddy and he nearly fell down. He felt even worse now. He wanted to turn and run away. But he remembered why he was there.

Paddy could see his da sitting at the kitchen table in his dressing gown, looking sad. He could see him trying to smile, like he was trying pick up a hundred-pound weight, as if his lips and mouth were too heavy. So Paddy kept running, but he picked up speed and ran ahead of Alice.

Alice tried to keep up with Paddy. But she couldn't. She'd wanted to say more to him, but she'd run out of breath after she'd said "No." She'd been going to add, "But I'd love to go to the pictures instead." Because Paddy had seemed to think the zoo was boring, the way he'd said, "Not interested" when she'd pointed out the snake house. But Paddy had run ahead of her before she'd had the chance.

Alice wanted to cry. She felt so tired and far from home, she just wanted to stop and walk away. But she kept running, because of her big brother, Luke. The Black Dog had been at Luke, stopping him from sleeping, stopping him from laughing and making Alice laugh the way he used to. The Black Dog had changed Luke—she'd heard her mammy say that—and Alice wanted the old Luke back. So she kept running.

The kids were still together, a big bunch of heads and elbows and knees. They ran past the red pandas and river hogs. There was a lot of noise in the air. The animals were waking up.

"The children are here!"

"Who said that?"

"Keep going. Come on!"

They were nearly at the elephant enclosure. They just had to run around one last sharp bend in the trail. The sudden corner made some of the kids laugh and bump into one another.

"Got yeh!"

"Got yeh back!"

"Got yeh back back!"

They got around that last corner. And then there was the shock.

The Black Dog was there.

Waiting for them.

They heard his howl before they saw him. It was a howl that ripped the zoo apart. Everything was gone. There was just the howl. A howl that stayed and became a word that hung there, like poisonous gas.

"USELESS!"

The fright made them quickly tired, exhausted. It seemed to suck up all the air. They'd been up all night. They'd been running for hours.

"USELESS!"

They sank to the ground. Raymond, Suzie, Damien, Gloria—all of them. They all lay down on the mucky trail. There was no talking, no protests, no animals hooting or roaring. The animal noise had suddenly stopped—dead. There was only the one word in the air.

"USELESS!"

Gloria's eyes were stinging and sad. They were closing. There was a word she needed, an important word, but she couldn't remember it. She couldn't remember anything. She had to sleep.

"USELESS!"

It was true. She was useless. She was too tired to do anything. Her eyes were so heavy and wet. She had to shut them. Just for a minute. That was all she had to do. That was all she could do. Because she was useless. She was doing that now, closing her eyes. She was . . . closing her eyes . . . now . . . for . . . ever.

"Excuse me!"

Gloria's eyes stopped closing. There was something pink. Waddling through the sleeping children. A flamingo. It was a flamingo. It was lots of flamingos. There was a big gang of pink flamingos, and they were marching up to the Dog. Gloria's eyes had started to close again. But—

"Excuse me!" said the first flamingo again.

Gloria could see the Dog now too. A big—a huge—angry dog. His eyes were red, and there was yellow stuff drooling from the sides of his mouth. He was staring down at the flamingo.

"Yes, you!" the flamingo yelled up at the Dog. "I'm talking to you! Some of us are trying to sleep, you know! We need our eight hours!"

"USELESS!"

"We're pink!" said the first flamingo. "Of course we're useless! That's the point!"

She was a Dublin flamingo.

"You eejit!"

Gloria smiled—she couldn't help it. A talking flamingo. It was—

"Brilliant," she said.

She remembered. That was the word she'd forgotten, the word she remembered she needed.

"Brilliant," she said again.

The flamingo's head turned on its long pink neck and the flamingo gawked at Gloria.

"Oh, thanks very much," said the flamingo—she was being sarcastic. "Too little, too late."

A sarcastic flamingo! It was—

"Brilliant," said Gloria.

The Dog seemed to move, to shift—to push away, lift its head.

"Wake up!" Gloria shouted. "Everyone! Come on! Wake up!"

She looked at the Dog. His eyes were even redder now, and furious. And his mouth—she couldn't even look at it. Its breath! She turned away. She couldn't face the Dog.

But she shouted. "Brilliant!"

She heard the groan—they all did—and the weight of the Dog seemed to lift off them. She saw the Dog's head move, pull away, farther and higher. It wasn't as close to her, and the disgusting breath was gone. The Dog was leaving.

"That's right!" said the first flamingo. "Go take a walk!"

"Or chase a ball!" said another.

"Under a car—hellohhhoh!"

Gloria started to laugh.

The other kids were waking up. Some of them were standing again. Some of them were yawning, one or two of them were crying. But they could see it, and feel it. The Black Dog was running away.

Alice crawled across the ground, to Paddy.

"Are you okay, Paddy?"

"Yeah," said Paddy. "What happened?"

"The Black Dog was here," said Alice. "Look!"

The Dog was running, charging, across the elephant

enclosure. Big clumps of muck shot into the air behind him as he ran. He was tearing the ground. The Dog was farther away now, but still huge, only a bit smaller than the adult elephants. They could feel the thump of his paws in the ground beneath them.

One of the elephants lifted its trunk and trumpeted: "Get out of our garden!"

"Oh God, Rayzer," said Gloria. "The elephants are talking now as well."

They watched the Dog run to the far edge of the enclosure, then jump. He stayed in the air for ages. It seemed like forever. Then he was over the high fence.

Gone.

"Come on!"

Raymond started to run, and the other kids followed. They were awake again. They'd survived, and they had the big word.

"Brilliant!"

They were winning again. They weren't tired now—they were full of oxygen and energy. And the energy, the power they felt in their legs and arms, came from the fact that they knew why they were running. They were going to get rid of the Black Dog for good. Then they'd go home to happier houses.

They ran back the way they'd come. They charged past the lake and the flamingos.

"This is a zoo—hellohhoh!" said a flamingo. "You're supposed to stop and look!"

Gloria shouted back at the flamingos. "You're gorgeous!"

"We know—hellohhoh! Go catch that brute of a dog!"

They were coming up to the meerkat enclosure.

"Go get him, kiddos!"

The meerkat was jumping up and down. But he couldn't reach the top of the wall.

"Come back to bed, Kevin," said his wife.

"I want to seeee!" he said. "Oh, I hope they are successful."

"Me too," said his wife. "They will try their best."

"Their vest?"

"Your ears are blocked again, Kevin."

"Perhaps, my love," said the meerkat. "But my eyesight is perfect, and your beauty makes my heart go jumpy-jumpy."

Kevin's wife tried to smile. She loved Kevin, but she was very depressed.

"Poor Kevin."

"No, no," said Kevin. "Rich Kevin! Expensive Kevin!"

The kids dashed past. Kevin looked back at the wall and shouted one last time. "Go get him, kiddos!"

"Who said that?" said Gloria.

She saw the top of a meerkat's head—

"'Twas meeeee!"

She saw the little head for just a second. Then he dropped back down to the grass of his enclosure. But she heard him again. They all did.

"I wish you successsssss!"

None of them stopped running, but all of them were amazed. She'd heard it before, but Gloria only now really understood. It dawned on her, and on the rest of the kids, just as the sun began to rise over Dublin.

"All the animals can talk!"

The meerkat, behind them, confirmed it.

"Yesss!" he shouted. "I never stop!"

He jumped again and tried to grab the top of the wall.

"Come back to bed, Kevin," said his wife.

"I want to go with the kiddos!"

"You have a job here," said his wife.

"But, my love!" said Kevin. "That Black Dog has made your life a misery! He has tormented you! He has filled you up with big unhappiness!"

He jumped again.

"Stay with me, Kevin," said his wife. "The children will defeat the Black Dog."

"But—!"

"And your job here is important," said Kevin's wife.

"Children love meerkats. Especially you."

Kevin stopped jumping.

"Only because they think I was in *The Lion King*," he said.

The kids were near the gate of the zoo. The air was full of the animals' messages. The grunts and chirps had become good luck wishes and shouts of encouragement.

"Catch him!"

"Bop him!"

"Bite his bum!"

It was brighter now, dawn, and the birds all around the park were working hard.

"Cheep, cheep! Cheaper, cheaper!"

"Are you not afraid of the daylight, Ernie?" asked Raymond.

"No way," said Ernie. "That's only an oul' myth."

"The Black Dog's afraid, though. Isn't he?"

"Maybe," said Ernie. "But I'm not convinced."

"Why not?" said Gloria.

"Dunno," said Ernie. "I can't work it out."

"More than just *brilliant*," said Raymond.

"Yeah," said Ernie. "It has to be. My dog, like—Fang. The only word he's afraid of is *bath*."

The zoo was open. There was a man, one of the zookeepers, opening the gate. He was yawning when he heard a noise and saw the huge gang of kids running straight at him. And his yawn became a silent scream.

Ernie stopped in front of him and showed him his fangs.

"Say your prayers, bud," said Ernie. "And wash your neck."

Then he ran after Raymond and Gloria. He shouted back at the zookeeper. "I'll be back."

The zookeeper held onto the gate—and his neck. He thought he was going to faint.

"Here, Mister," said Paddy. "Do we have to pay to get out?"

The zookeeper had breath left for one word. "No."

"Seeyeh, so," said Paddy, and he kept running.

Alice was beside him. She thought it was the funniest thing she'd ever heard. She wanted to tell Paddy that, but she needed all her breath to keep up.

The kids all ran past the zookeeper.

They were gone.

Early-morning life seemed to be back to normal, although the animals inside were making a lot more noise than usual. All sorts of grunts and yaps and howls and barks and chatter. The zookeeper would go in now and shout at them.

But the kids—the sight and the sound of all those kids, their excitement. It had reminded the zookeeper of something. He remembered now. He used to sing to the animals every morning. Before the Black Dog started visiting his house.

He'd forgotten that, like he'd forgotten how to sing.

He remembered something else now, something that cheeky kid with the black cape had said to him. He could still see the kids, the last of them, running out of the Park. He put his hands to his mouth, made a trumpet, and shouted.

"I did wash my neck!"

CHAPTER 10

It was very early morning in the city of
Dublin, and people lying awake in bed could hear a
sound that every Dubliner likes, a ship's foghorn out
on Dublin Bay. But there was something else they could
hear too. The birds. The city's birds were often noisy, but this
was different. It was like the War of the Birds out there, with all
the cawing and squawking, and the seagulls seemed to be on the
side that was winning.

But most people were still asleep. It was Saint Patrick's Day,
Ireland's big holiday, so there was no school and nearly every
adult who had a job didn't have to go to work. Alarm clocks
and phone alarms were turned off, and even the babies seemed
to know that they didn't have to start crying and complaining
until later than usual.

But the kids were wide awake. They were out of Phoenix
Park by now, and they were running toward the center of town,

along the quays, beside the River Liffey. There were hardly any cars or trucks, and the few adults they saw walking looked tired and cold, as if they'd been walking all night.

They were still chasing the Black Dog. But—

"Where is he?" asked Precious.

He'd had been in front of them, a few corners ahead. But then he was gone. Again.

He seemed to be playing a game with them, leading them on, teasing them.

They all slowed down, unsure, disappointed, relieved— worried. Was this another of the Black Dog's tricks?

"Is he hiding?"

"Where's he gone?"

"Keep going!" Damien shouted.

"Yeah!" Raymond agreed.

If they stopped now, they probably wouldn't be able start again. Their legs would feel stiff and their feet would be sore. They had to keep running.

They heard a voice.

"He's down there, so he is!"

It seemed to have come from way above them. Gloria looked up as she ran, but all she could see was a gang of seagulls. Then they heard the voice again.

"There!"

It was lower this time, to her right. She looked, and saw a seagull flying beside them, over the river.

"Just follow my beak!"

"Oh my God!" said Alice. "The seagull's talking."

"Well, the pink birds in the zoo were talking as well," said Paddy. "So, it's no big deal, like."

The seagull had gone ahead, flying faster than they'd ever seen a seagull fly before. No floating or gliding, his wings were going mad, like a colossal wasp's.

"I thought seagulls would be too stupid to talk," said Alice.

There was a sudden squawk, right in her ear. It was another seagull, flying beside Alice's shoulder.

"You got that one wrong, love!" the seagull roared at Alice. "See him—see him, do yeh?!"

The second seagull's beak was pointing at the first seagull, flying ahead of them.

"Yeah," said Alice.

It was the first time she'd ever spoken to a seagull.

"Well, he's my fella!"

"Really?"

"He's me life partner!"

"Oh," said Alice. "So you're a girl, then?"

The seagull stared at Alice. She was brilliant at it, considering she was flying straight into the wind.

"Is it not obvious?!" she eventually squawked, after six very long seconds.

"Eh . . ."

"And you think *we're* stupid?!" she squawked. "My God!"

And she flew after her boyfriend. "Pete!" she cawed. "Wait up!"

(Try cawing "Pete." It isn't easy.)

They saw it now—they understood. All the seagulls were

flying with them. That was how it seemed anyway, and how it looked. Every seagull in Dublin seemed to be above or beside them. It was like running inside a tunnel made of seagulls. It should have been terrifying. But it wasn't. The seagulls were with them, encouraging them.

"Keep it up!"

"Yis're doin' great!"

"Considerin' yis don't have wings!"

"Or proper beaks!"

The kids kept running, past Collins Barracks. There was still no sign of the Dog. But the seagull at the front was still pointing straight ahead, along the river. He flew under the James Joyce Bridge.

"Wheee!"

"Pete! Wait, will yeh!"

Gloria loved the seagulls. She remembered once when she went to a place with her Uncle Ben. Raymond wasn't with them, or her mam or dad. It was just Gloria and Uncle Ben. They'd gone in his van to this amazing place. He'd called it the South Wall. But it wasn't really a wall. It was more like a wide path, and it went right into the sea. It took more than half an hour for them to walk to the end of it, and the sea was on both sides of them all the way. It was like they were walking out of Ireland, across a bridge that grew out as they walked. The sea was rough on one side, and calm on the other, rough where the sea stretched out to the rest of the world, calm where the wall—maybe it was a wall, after all—blocked the waves and protected the bay and the docks. The sunshine bounced on the sea, and the

sky was full of seagulls. They were mad. It looked like they were playing football, with hundreds on each team—and no ball.

As Gloria and her uncle got nearer to the red lighthouse at the end of the wall—okay, it was a wall—she saw why the gulls were going mad, swooping and dive-bombing. There were loads of men fishing there, pulling fish out of the water, and throwing the little ones back in.

"They're like kids in a sweetshop," said Uncle Ben.

"Deadly," said Gloria. "Chocolate-coated mackerel."

"That's not a bad idea," said Uncle Ben.

There was a ship, one of the ferries, coming into Dublin Bay. It seemed so close, Gloria only had to lean out a bit to touch its side as it glided past.

"Oh my God!"

The Dog was there, in front of them. He was at the corner of Smithfield. Gloria knew the name of the place because she'd been there loads of times with her dad. The Dog was right in front of them. "No more daydreaming," she said to herself. "Concentrate."

It was like the Dog had been in front of them all along, but the glare of the morning's early sunshine had made him impossible to see. But now he was back. And he wasn't running away this time. He was coming toward them.

"Uh-oh!"

The Dog's head lifted slowly to stare right at them. It was colossal, the head, as big as the whole Dog had been when they'd chased him out of Phoenix Park. He started to open his mouth.

His teeth were dripping, his tongue looked hard and horrible.

Gloria knew what was happening. She knew what they had to do.

"Quick!" she yelled. "Shout before he does! Brilliant!"

Nothing happened. *Brilliant* wasn't working. It was proper daylight now, so *brilliant* didn't explode into light, the way it had in the night. It was just a word.

Some of the kids slowed down, and the seagulls scattered all over the sky. Other kids stopped, too frightened to go any further. But Gloria kept running at the Dog. So did Raymond and Ernie. And Damien. And others too—Paddy, Alice, Sunday, Suzie, Precious.

Gloria knew now that the Black Dog wasn't afraid of the light. The air was bright and kind of lovely, but the Dog had never looked fiercer. His eyes were huge; the light wasn't making him squint or cringe. He didn't care about the light. He never had. Their weapon—*brilliant*—was no good to them.

But Gloria wasn't going to give up.

Brilliant!

It had worked before. Something in the word—maybe not the light—had sent the Dog running away. So she kept running at him and she kept shouting.

"Brilliant!"

There was nothing else to do.

The Dog still came at them. His eyes were dark caves. There was no shine in them, no twinkle.

Gloria didn't look at the Dog's eyes. She kept running—they

all kept running—straight for the mouth, which seemed to be growing bigger and deeper. And lower. The Dog was bringing its head down, nearer to the street. The kids were more and more frightened, but the fear seemed to pull them closer to the thing that frightened them. They were so close now, they could smell his breath. It wasn't dog breath—it wasn't normal dog breath. It was—

"Socks!" shouted Precious.

They couldn't help laughing, even though they were scared.

"Brilliant!"

Just for a second, it had made the Dog seem silly, the smell of old socks coming out of his huge, angry mouth.

"Feet!" shouted Suzie.

"Brilliant!"

The Black Dog's mouth had stopped growing. He was standing still.

They charged straight at him.

"Brilliant!!"

The word was working—something about it. Gloria quickly looked up at the Dog's eyes and saw him blink, just once. He was turning sideways, to get away.

From what—what was he trying to escape from? It wasn't the kids. It couldn't have been—they were only kids. Raymond looked around. There were hundreds of them, and there were even more coming, to join the ones who'd been running all night. But the kids alone weren't disturbing the Dog. And it wasn't the light. What was it?

Gloria had been thinking too as she ran.

"It's the word he hates!" she shouted. "Not the light."

The Black Dog was up on his hind legs. Then he fell backwards and landed on his front paws and charged away, down Arran Quay. The kids saw what was happening and kept running, faster now, because the Dog was running away.

"BRILLIANT!"

Alice had an idea.

"Maybe it's not just the word," she said. "It's what the word means."

"Yeah," said Gloria, although she was a bit annoyed; she'd been going to say that. "The Black Dog hates anything brilliant."

"The Black Dog hates *everything* brilliant," said Alice.

Paddy made sure he was running right beside Alice.

"That was cool," he said.

Alice thought she'd start to fly. She'd never felt so happy, so light, so full of joy. Even though she was sweating and the label on her knickers was itching her as she ran.

"Thanks," she said—or she meant to say. But "Label" was what she actually said. She couldn't believe it!

But Paddy didn't seem to mind, or hear. He smiled at her. And she smiled at him. They couldn't stop smiling at each other. Neither of them wanted to be the first to stop.

The Black Dog's paws smashed down on the street. They could feel the weight, the vibration in their feet as they ran. And he was getting even bigger. He was so wide now he filled most of the street.

"Not so brilliant," said Ernie. "What d'you think, bud?" he asked Raymond.

"Not sure," said Raymond.

The Dog was definitely expanding. But—

"He's still running away," said Damien.

"Good point," said Ernie. And he shouted as he ran.

"Chicken!"

Most of the kids started laughing. It was mad, calling a dog a chicken. A lot of them joined in.

"Chicken!!"

Gloria wasn't too sure that calling the Dog a chicken was such a good idea.

"He might feel insulted," said Gloria.

"That's the idea," said Ernie.

"He might get angrier," said Gloria.

"That's the idea," said Ernie.

"He might turn around and charge at us," said Gloria.

"That's not the idea," said Ernie.

"Chicken!!"

"Shut up!" said Ernie.

"Brilliant!" Gloria shouted, and all the kids joined in.

The Dog's fur rubbed the sides of buildings as he ran. The kids heard a strange sound, a bit like an animal crying out in pain or protest. But it wasn't an animal. It was the iron railings in front of the Four Courts. By the time the kids ran past, they could see that the Dog, the weight and the size of him, had bent and twisted the railings as he'd gone past.

That scared the kids. They were silent now as they ran.

Ernie had an idea.

"Okay," he shouted, and flapped his cape. "Yis listenin'? Shout if these things are brilliant. Ice cream is—"

"Brilliant!"

"Chips are —"

"Brilliant!"

They were laughing again. Happy and terrified—it was a great combination. They were full of new energy, bursting with the stuff.

"Christmas is—"

"Brilliant!"

"School is—"

"Crap!"

"Oh yeah," said Ernie. "I forgot. Movin' on. Chasin' after dogs is—"

"Brilliant!"

"I can't hear yis!"

"BRILL-iant!"

"Wha'?!"

"Brill-IANT!!"

"Still I can't hear yis!"

"BRILLIANT!"

The seagulls were back in action, flying all around and above them.

"Go on," they squawked. "Go on, go on, go on!"

Gloria loved their faces, the way they managed to look bored and excited at the exact same time. The seagulls looked intelligent, like they probably read books when they weren't catching fish or rooting in bins. And she thought now that they might be able to answer a question that had been nudging her all night.

"Why us?" she shouted at one of them.

Before the seagull could answer, Gloria saw another amazing thing. A fish—she thought it was a salmon, but she wasn't sure. She didn't know much about fish, except she didn't like the taste of them. Anyway, the fish had just jumped out of the water, high enough for Gloria to see him shining in the sun. She saw his mouth. She heard the words.

"Good luck!"

"A talking fish," said Gloria.

"Big deal," said the seagull.

"Why us?" Gloria asked again.

The seagull swooped away and held herself in the wind for a while, her wings still. Then she swooped back down to Gloria.

"That was nice," she said. "I was getting sweaty under my wings. Why what?"

"Why kids?" said Gloria. "You're kind of supporting us, aren't you? All of you seagulls. And the animals in the zoo. And now the fish. Why?"

"Is it not obvious?" said the seagull.

"No."

"The Black Dog of Depression hates kids."

"Why?"

"You're the future," said the seagull, and she swooped away.

"Hear that, Ernie?" said Gloria.

"Wha'?"

"We're the future," said Gloria.

"Groovy," said Ernie.

Gloria liked the word *future*. She often lay in bed and planned her future. Or she baked with her mam and smelled her future—she'd be a baker, or a chef, a celebrity chef who smiled and never shouted. Things she did now—now— would make her future. And not just her future, *the* future— everyone's. And not just Gloria, all the kids here—the seagull had said it. They were making the future by chasing the Black Dog.

But what if they couldn't catch him? What would the future be like then?

The seagull had swooped back down.

"Look out!" she said. "He's trying to get away."

Gloria could see the Dog turning. He'd grown too big to do it quickly. They all saw him turn left onto Capel Street. They heard his fur scraping corner bricks. They heard window glass breaking. The sound of the glass hitting the street was frightening, but the noise of the Dog's hair on the corner bricks was worse. It was high-pitched, like nails on a blackboard, something they could feel as well as hear. It was like a warning, like they were running into an earthquake just before it started. But the kids kept running.

They ran over the broken window glass as they turned the corner. There was heat in the air, kind of wet and horrible, and the hair the Dog had left behind seemed to surround them, stroke them, scratch them. The kids with asthma felt as if a huge wet hand had grabbed their lungs. Other kids were coughing and wheezing.

"Keep going!" Raymond shouted.

They'd to be able to run through the hair, he thought—he hoped. They'd escape to fresh air on the other side. If they just kept going.

But the kids were struggling. The breath was being pulled from their lungs by the wet hand—that was what it felt like. Some of the kids had to stop; they'd no breath left. They'd never get through. They just couldn't breathe.

But the seagulls rescued them. They were suddenly everywhere around the kids. They flapped their wings and scattered the dog hair. It was like someone had turned on an enormous fan. The kids could feel the air on their faces. They could safely open their mouths and breathe. They could open their eyes and see one of the most amazing things they'd ever see. (But not *the* most amazing thing. That would come later.) The street, the sky, the whole world was full of flapping seagulls—and every other bird in Dublin. That was what it looked like. Every magpie, robin, every cormorant and oystercatcher, crow and heron was flying around them, making the air fresh and cool. There were thousands of birds, huge to tiny, an army of squawks and peeps. There was even a ladybird.

"I'm a bird, not a bug!"

But none of them collided. They swooped and climbed and dived. One of the seagulls flew past Paddy, backwards.

"Here's one for YouTube!" the seagull squawked.

The kids were going again. Their lungs were full of the best of air. They were ready to run and shout.

"Brilliant!"

"Thanks," said Gloria.

"You're welcome," said a seagull. "But you're on your own now, love. This is as far as we can go."

The other birds dropped back or flew up and away. The kids were alone again, an army of them, running after the Dog.

"Come on!"

Raymond was at the front, with Damien beside him, and Ernie.

"God, I'm starvin'," said Ernie.

"Hey, Rayzer," Gloria shouted. "Ernie's staring at your neck."

Raymond put his hands up, to save his neck from Ernie's fangs. "Stay away from me!"

"I was only messing," said Gloria.

They started laughing as they ran.

There was a rat standing on the corner of Mary Street.

"See?" said the rat. "That's why the Black Dog hates you."

"Why?" said Alice.

She'd never really spoken to a rat before.

"Because you're laughing when you should be crying," said the rat.

The rat pointed.

"He went that way, by the way."

"Thanks."

"You're welcome," said the rat. "We're quite nice, us rats. Don't listen to the media."

"Okay."

The Dog had turned onto Mary Street. The kids heard the crunch of corner bricks again. They charged around the corner, over the rubble and glass. The Dog's paws on the street, the hundreds of kids' shoes, the shouting, hundreds and hundreds of children's voices—the noise was unbelievable.

The Black Dog was on Henry Street by now, heading straight for the Spire, the huge steel needle-shaped sculpture in the middle of the street. Then he lifted. He took off, exactly like a plane. He rose slowly, a colossal dog-shaped cloud, too dark for rain or anything normal. He sailed over O'Connell Street, over the Spire. He sailed over the statue of Big Jim Larkin, whose colossal hands seemed to reach up to grab the Dog.

But the Dog was too high up.

The kids stopped at the Spire. They were exhausted, and thirsty.

"Do we have to keep going?" one of them asked. "He's floating away, sure."

"Yeah," said Gloria. "We do. He has Dublin's funny bone, remember."

"Oh yeah. I forgot."

They all remembered now. The Black Dog might have been

floating away—and a lot of them hoped he was. But he still had the funny bone. The city's supply of laughter was in the bone—all of the city's future happy times, Gloria thought—and they had to get it back.

But it was hard to tell which way to go. The Black Dog seemed to be spreading out. The cloud was getting wider and thicker.

"How do we follow that?" said Damien. "He's all over the place."

Damien was worried. He'd had a toothache earlier that he'd thought had gone away. But it hadn't.

Raymond wanted to start running again. So did Gloria and Ernie, and most of the others. But the Dog was covering more and more of the city. The kids could feel his weight on top of them. They began to understand what being depressed might feel like. They could see grown-up people along O'Connell Street, sitting on the ground, holding their heads.

The cloud had made the city center very dark. Raymond didn't like that.

"Here!" he roared. "Shout *Brilliant!*"

There were more kids now than ever before.

"BRILLIANT!"

The light from the word was explosive. It lit up the street and the sky above it. It was great to see what the word could do again.

"BRILLIANT!"

And it worked. The cloud started to shift, to move away, north, over Talbot Street and Connolly Station, over the Five Lamps, East Wall, and Fairview.

"He's trying to get away from the light!" Raymond shouted. "Come on!"

They were stiff, tired, thirsty. But they pushed the pains and aches away. The more they moved, the quicker they got. They charged down Talbot Street.

Years later, when they thought back to that night and morning, they would never really understand how they'd been able to run so far and for so long. Now, though, they just kept running. More kids joined in, kids who'd been running all night as well, coming from other parts of the city, maybe even the rest of Ireland. Thousands of kids ran down Amiens Street, along the North Strand, through Fairview, and under the railway bridge. They could see the sea now, Dublin Bay, right in front of them, and the wind suddenly bashed them, whacked them, as if it had been hiding behind the railway bridge.

They laughed.

"Cool!"

It wasn't all that funny, but they remembered what the rat had told them, how the Dog hated it when kids laughed. So they spread out their arms and ran straight at the wind.

"Ha-ha!"

They pretended they were the seagulls. They felt the wind push against their chests. They leaned forward a bit and let the wind hold them up. Most of them knew where they were—Clontarf. They could see the Hill of Howth miles ahead, and the docks were to the right, not that far away. They saw the two big chimneys of the Poolbeg power station. And Gloria saw it, tiny in the distance, the red lighthouse she'd walked to with

Uncle Ben, the day they'd watched the seagulls playing football in the sky. It reminded her of why she was there.

"Come on!" she shouted.

"This way!" Raymond shouted as the exact same time.

They laughed at that, and ran. They stopped being seagulls and became kids again. This was serious. They could see the Dog. There was no way they couldn't have seen him. He was covering all of Dublin Bay, the darkest cloud they'd ever seen.

"Come on!"

They ran after Raymond.

Raymond remembered once, when he'd been here with his

Uncle Ben. He'd had his bike in the back of Uncle Ben's van. They'd taken it out, and Raymond had biked on the bike path. Uncle Ben had timed him, and Raymond had gone a few seconds faster every time. They'd bought ice creams from the snack shop. Raymond could see the shop now, the Costa, just across the road. Then they got back into the van to go home. And Uncle Ben's ice cream had fallen out of his cone, right into his lap, when he was turning left, driving out of the car park. They'd laughed all the way back to Raymond's house. It had just been Raymond and Uncle Ben.

The cloud was getting thicker, and it seemed to be lower in the sky, almost low enough to touch. But none of the kids wanted to touch it. It looked too solid as it rolled and squirmed and slid.

"It's like a snake," said Alice.

Paddy didn't answer. Even just the word *snake* made his mouth go dry.

Gloria had caught up with Raymond.

"Hey, Rayzer," she said. "Remember the time we were here with Uncle Ben?"

"No," said Raymond.

"You do," said Gloria. "Uncle Ben's ice cream fell into his lap. Remember?"

"You weren't there."

"Yes, I was."

They were running right beside the sea, along the path that the grown-ups called the Promenade. The tide was in and the wind was strong, loud and packed with drops of seawater.

"No, you weren't."

"I was so."

"You weren't there for the ice cream."

"Yes, I was."

"Here," said Ernie. "Yis can have your ice cream war another time."

"Sorry, Ernie," said Raymond. "BRILLIANT!"

Spray from the waves flew at them, like freezing spit. Their faces were sore from the cold.

Damien had dropped back a bit because of his toothache. It was really sore, and he'd been afraid that if he spoke his words would come out like baby talk. But now his face, his whole head, was freezing and numb. It was great.

"My head's a toothache!" he shouted into the wind.

The kids around him laughed and joined in.

"My head's a toothache!"

They watched the dog cloud buckle and twist, becoming less like a cloud, much more like the Dog.

"My head's an earache!"

They were running alongside the sea, but they weren't getting any nearer to the Dog.

"My head's a pancake!"

"Your bum's a face ache!"

But then they came to the wooden bridge that went out to Bull Island, the big beach in the middle of Dublin Bay. Now they could run straight at the Dog. They knew—they felt it: This was the last fight.

The Battle of Clontarf.

Raymond stopped, and waited till all the kids had gathered together. There were thousands of them. Every kid in Dublin seemed to be there and they were all at the wooden bridge, packed together.

Waiting.

Raymond pointed at the Dog and shouted as loud as he could.

"Charge!"

The kids cheered—they all did, and they ran onto the bridge. A long line of children ran over the old wooden boards—*trip, trap, trip, trap.*

"Who's that tripping over my bridge?" roared the troll as he climbed out from under the bridge. "Wazzup?"

"We're huntin' dog blood, bud," said Ernie.

"The Black Dog of Depression?" said the troll.

"That's the one," said Ernie.

"Cool," said the troll. "He's been depressing my mammy." And he ran beside Ernie.

"How's business?" Ernie asked him.

"Slow enough," said the troll. "But it should pick up nearer the summer."

The noise on the bridge was amazing. All those feet stomping on the wood. It made them brave. They sounded like the world's biggest army, even though lots of the feet were very small.

"My tooth's an earache!"

They were off the bridge now. They missed the sound and the bounce of the wood under their feet. They were running on cement and sand now. The sound of their feet was drowned by the roar of the wind and the waves.

They ran past the golf club, past the old changing shelters, straight into the gale and the gloom—

"Brilliant!"

They ran all the way down to the beach. And they stopped. They couldn't run any farther. There was no more land. They were on the edge of Dublin and the Black Dog was right over them.

"What'll we do?"

"Don't know."

They hadn't really thought about it. How were they going to catch him?

"Anyone bring a ladder?" said Paddy, but not even Alice laughed.

As if the Dog had heard Paddy's joke, strings of cloud twirled slowly and began to look like huge snakes dangling right over him.

And the cloud dropped slowly—it was definitely lower. The sea had disappeared. There was solid, rolling fog in front of them.

But how could they attack him?

It annoyed, and worried, Raymond. They'd come this far and now he couldn't think of anything to do.

"Look," said Ernie. "He's up to somethin'—see?"

The Dog was turning—the cloud was starting to move. His fur was rolling, growing. A cloud seemed to grow out of the main cloud, and became his head and face. And it was staring back the way they'd come, at the city.

He snarled.

"USELESS."

The ground seemed to shake under them.

Raymond knew what was happening—he suddenly knew it.

"It's a trap!" he shouted.

The Black Dog had dragged the kids away from the city and now he was going back, to destroy it. He was going to drop down onto the whole city—he was big enough to do it now—and smother it, and all the adults under him. He'd make their lives unbearable. And the kids would be left alone, crowded here on Dollymount Strand, unable to do anything about it, except watch.

They thought they heard a deep, horrible laugh.

"Fooled you," said the Dog—his voice filled the air. "You thought you were great, didn't you? Chasing me. 'You're the future.' Have you stopped me, little children?"

They watched the cloud grow and darken. It became an even more definite, solid shape. It was the Black Dog of Depression, the most horrible thing they'd ever seen. The Dog's hairs were thousands of snakes. Their heads—and tongues—were all around him, flicking and sneering.

He was moving away.

"You're all USELESS."

Gloria knew. If they heard the word again, they'd believe

what the Dog was telling them. They'd lie down on the sand. The sea would roll over them.

One or two of the kids had already started to lie down.

"Shout!" she roared. "Shout! Brilliant!"

The wind grabbed Gloria's words and seemed to stop them from going far. But Suzie heard her.

"Brilliant!"

And so did Alice and Sunday and Precious.

"Brilliant!"

Damien's toothache was back, and worse. He opened his mouth, but the cold air was agony. It went straight for his tooth. But he knew why he was there. He opened his mouth again, took a deep painful breath, and—

"Brilliant!"

All the kids were shouting now.

Every kid shouted—one huge shout.

"BRILLIANT!"

And it was working. The word and what it meant was starting to hit the Black Dog.

"My head's a toothache!"

"BRILLIANT!"

The Dog was curling, buckling. But he was still moving, escaping. He was floating back to the city, and their parents and uncles, big brothers and sisters.

"What'll we do? We can't shout any louder."

"He's not afraid enough."

"Ernie!" Raymond shouted.

"Wha'?"

"We're going in."

"Wha'?!"

The wind was howling. The sand stung their faces, and it was getting even darker.

"We're going in there," Raymond shouted.

He pointed at the lowest part of the Dog, the fog that was hanging over the sea.

"Right into the Dog," said Raymond.

"You're jestin'," said Ernie.

"I'm not," said Raymond.

He wished he was joking. He was asking Ernie to take him into the darkest place there was, the core—the very center—of the Black Dog. The thing that frightened him more than anything else, and the most frightening thing he could possibly do.

"Fair enough," said Ernie.

He grabbed the back of Raymond's hoodie.

"Anythin' for a laugh," said Ernie, although he wasn't laughing.

Paddy stepped forward.

"Me as well," he said.

Paddy looked at the Black Dog. He forced himself to do it. He looked at the thousands of squirming snakes. He could see them all. Waiting for him.

He didn't have to do it.

But he did. Paddy knew why he was there.

Ernie held onto Paddy's collar.

"Here we go."

Ernie started to drift across the sand.

"Hate this," he said.

Fast this time, faster—he gathered speed, and the rest of the kids watched as Ernie, with Paddy and Raymond, shot straight at the cloud, and into it.

They waited.

"Keep shouting!" roared Gloria.

Raymond couldn't see. He couldn't see anything. Not a thing. He was buried. Freezing. He couldn't open his mouth— he didn't have a mouth. He didn't know where he was—or why he was. He knew nothing.

But he heard a voice. Near him. Ernie.

"We'll be grand, we'll be grand. Just a few more seconds."

Ernie's voice was right at Raymond's ear.

"D'you know why I'm doin' this?" said Ernie.

Raymond forced the word through his freezing lips: "Why?"

"For my da," said Ernie.

They were still moving. Paddy could feel it, the movement. He'd shut his eyes, but he could feel himself charging through the rolling snakes. He thought they were going up now, Paddy, Raymond, and Ernie—like they were climbing up the snakes' backs or something. But he could feel nothing under his feet.

"Everyone says he's a waster," said Ernie. "But they don't know him. He's a great da. The way he was before the Dog got to him."

Ernie coughed.

"So, that's why I'm here," he said. "Here goes."

Raymond and Paddy heard Ernie.

"BRILLIANT, BRILLIANT, bleedin' BRILLIANT!"

Down on the beach the kids couldn't see the three boys anymore. They were inside the Dog—they'd disappeared completely.

They waited. It felt like ages. Minutes.

Then they heard the voice from inside the cloud.

"BRILLIANT, BRILLIANT, bleedin' BRILLIANT!"

It seemed to come from miles away. But they'd heard it.

"That was Ernie," said Gloria.

"Brilliant!"

They shouted as hard as they could. But the wind grabbed their voices. They had no breath left. They watched, and waited—and hoped. They could still hear Ernie, and Paddy and Raymond, in the sky above them.

". . . brilliant . . . brilliant . . ."

But the shouts seemed to come from farther away.

"Look!"

They could see chinks now, tiny holes appearing in the cloud. Sunlight was getting through, narrow little beams of it.

Raymond saw the light, but he had no strength left, no voice. Paddy saw the light hit the snakes, saw the snakes start to fade. But he was so cold. He felt like he was frozen in ice. He just wanted to sleep forever.

"Here!" said Ernie. "Don't tell me you're bored. Wake up!"

Paddy remembered the word.

"Brilliant."

"Good man," said Ernie. "Louder, but."

"Brilliant," said Raymond.

One of the holes in the cloud got bigger, wider. He thought he could see the sun.

The kids were drenched and freezing. They could hear the boys way up in the Dog—they could just about hear them. But that stopped too. There was just the wind. The holes in the cloud were filling in.

They heard the Dog.

"Useless . . ."

"Oh, no."

But Gloria noticed: The Dog wasn't loud this time. He was tiring too. The kids could still win, if they were quick enough. But the wind was charging all around, blowing stinging sand straight at them. Gloria put her fingers in front of her mouth like a mask and she inhaled as much air as she could.

"One more time!" she shouted.

All the kids copied Gloria. They protected their faces with their hands and sleeves, and breathed in deep. They inhaled the wind and they sent it down to their lungs.

Damien couldn't open his mouth. It was too sore. But he grabbed a stick and jumped up on a rock. Then, just like the conductor of an orchestra, he held his arms and the stick in the air. The wind tried to knock him off the rock. But it couldn't. Damien wasn't going to be bullied by the wind.

All the kids looked at him. They knew what he was doing. They held their breath—they waited.

Damien the conductor dropped his arms.

And the kids let go of the air. They fired it straight up at the Dog.

"BRILLIANNNNNNT!"

And it worked. The word ripped through the cloud. The holes were big again, and they could see sky. The Dog was breaking, becoming smaller, harmless clouds.

But that stopped. The clouds stayed together, remained one cloud.

And it snarled. The snarl came from a mouth and the mouth was holding something very big and white.

The funny bone.

Gloria was ready.

The boys in the cloud saw the funny bone. It wasn't as dark in there and the snakes had faded away. They should have been less frightened. But what they saw now was even worse. The funny bone was being held by teeth—real, sharp teeth. They were inside the jaws of the Dog. The cloud, all around them, was becoming solid—and fleshy.

"We're standing on his tongue," said Raymond.

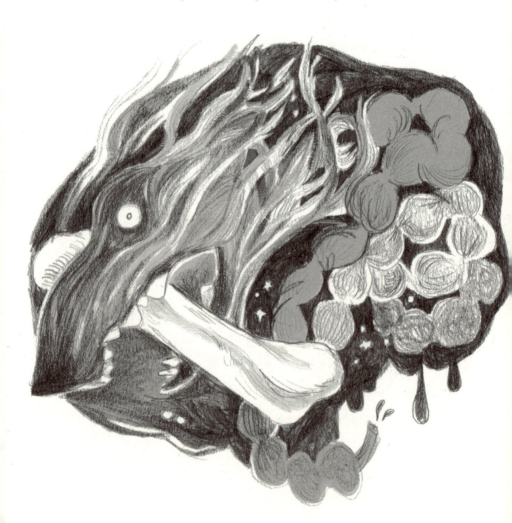

"He's going to swallow us!" Paddy yelled.

"He's not swallowin' me," said Ernie.

The boys felt Ernie strengthen his grip on their clothes, and they flew across the tongue and the Dog's drool. They charged up to the bone, right up against the back of the Dog's teeth.

Ernie let go of Paddy and Raymond.

"Push!"

Gloria had kept some breath, just enough for one last small—

". . . brilliant . . ."

It was enough.

The word—the light, the tiny bit of desperate happiness—hit the cloud and the Black Dog exploded.

It just disappeared. One minute, there was the gale and the colossal snarling Dog. Next, there was silence—nothing. Except blue sky and quiet.

And guts.

"Oh my God!"

"Run!"

They ran to the dunes to get away. They heard the guts fall, slapping the sand like hard-boiled rain. They heard the shouts of three screaming boys.

"Look out below!"

Raymond held onto Ernie's waist while Ernie held his parachute-cape in one hand and the back of Paddy's pants with the other.

"Let go!" Paddy yelled.

"Don't think so, bud," said Ernie. "Even sand is hard when you fall this far."

The kids below saw something else, something big and white, and—

"Oh my God again!"

They ran even farther away, into the dunes, even into the water. They heard the thump—they felt it. It lifted some of them off the ground.

They turned, and saw Dublin's funny bone. It was lying on

the beach, white and bright and kind of funny. Exactly like a city's funny bone should have looked.

Ernie, hanging on to Paddy and Raymond, landed beside it in the sand. He stood up and shook the guts off his cape.

"Nothin' to it," he said.

The air was suddenly full of seagulls and, a minute later, there was no sign of the guts or the Dog. There were no seagulls in the air. They were too full to fly. They were waddling around like drunk robots.

One of them waddled past Gloria.

"Never again," it said.

"Are you a girl or a boy?" Gloria asked.

"Is it not obvious, like?"

"Girl?"

The seagull nodded.

"Never again," she said. "I'll stick to the veg."

She stopped waddling and pointed her beak at the funny bone.

"Good job," she said.

"Thanks," said Gloria.

Ernie was leaning against the funny bone. Hundreds of kids were climbing all over it.

"So this is the funny bone," said Gloria.

"Looks like it."

"Where are all the laughs?"

"Inside in the marrow," said Raymond.

Damien was standing on top of the bone. He got down on his knees and put his ear to the bone.

"Shake it," he said.

Dozen of kids started pushing the bone, making it rock in the sand. The kids on the bone held on or fell off.

"Hear anything?"

They all heard it, like the sound came from deep inside a cave. It was laughter.

"Ah, deadly!" said Gloria. "The funny bone's laughing."

Everybody started laughing, including the bloated seagulls. Damien stood up on the bone.

"Hey!" he yelled. "My toothache's gone!"

Then they heard a voice. They thought they did—it seemed to come from inside the bone.

"Do you want it back?"

"No, thanks!" said Damien.

Ernie was still leaning against the bone.

"What'll we do with this thing?" he said.

"Don't worry," said one of the seagulls. "The city will take it back."

"How?"

He hadn't finished speaking when he fell onto the sand. The funny bone had disappeared.

"That's how," said the seagull. "It's back where it should be. Inside the city, like. Everything will get back to normal now. Except my stummick."

addy climbed onto the garden wall. Then he made the jump to the shed roof. The jump was easy, but he always worried that the roof would cave in and he'd fall into the shed.

But he landed safely, not too loudly. He waited a second—he listened.

"8654326," he whispered.

He was trying to remember Alice's phone number. He'd been whispering it all the way home from the beach. He was afraid he'd dropped a number or two on the way—he wasn't sure. He'd phone her when he got into the house.

"8654326."

He stretched his arms and grabbed his bedroom windowsill. He pulled himself up till his arms were resting on the sill. He'd left the window very slightly open, so he was able to pull it toward him with one his hands. It creaked—but only a tiny bit.

"8654326."

He held onto the open window and pulled himself up. His knee, then both knees were on the windowsill. He carefully stood, bent his head, and climbed into his bedroom.

"8654326," he whispered. "8654326."

"That sounds like a girl's phone number," said a voice.

Paddy nearly died—he nearly fell backwards out the window.

It was his da, and he was standing in Paddy's room.

And he was smiling.

Really smiling.

And he was dressed in proper clothes. It was ages since Paddy had seen his da like this. He thought of the funny bone on the beach, sinking back into the city, and he laughed.

And so did his da.

"Will you ever start using the door, Paddy?"

Paddy shrugged.

"I do," he said. "Sometimes."

His da laughed again.

"I was thinking," he said. "Remember we always went up to the mountains on Saint Patrick's Day?"

"Yeah," said Paddy.

"Well," said his da. "Will we do it again—today? All of us. We can bring a bit of a picnic."

Paddy wasn't fully convinced he was awake.

"Cool," he said. "Yeah."

He sat on the bed, and his da sat beside him. His da stayed there, real, smelling of aftershave or something. He put his arm around Paddy's shoulders.

"Do you want to make that phone call before we go?" he asked.

"What phone call?" said Paddy.

"The number you were whispering when you came through the window."

"Oh," said Paddy. "Yeah."

He was blushing—he could feel his face burning. His da was grinning at him.

"Oh, no," said Paddy.

"What's wrong, son?"

"I've forgotten it."

"No problem," said his da. "It's 8654326."

And he started laughing.

• • •

Alice was starving. But she couldn't eat. There was a special Paddy's Day breakfast right under her nose, and a special Paddy's voice still ringing in her ears. But she couldn't think of Paddy or smell the sausages and rashers.

Because of Luke. Her big brother.

He was holding two sausages on two forks, one in each hand, and he was pretending the sausages were having a conversation.

"I am not made of pig!" a sausage protested.

"Yes, you are," said the other. "Get over it."

The show—it *was* a show—had been going on for ten minutes, since Luke strolled into the kitchen and smiled at Alice and her mam—for the first time in months.

"I'm not a pig! I'm a sausage!"

"Look at the packet. What's that animal on the packet?"

"It's a cartoon!"

"Of a pig."

"No! It can't be true!"

It was the old Luke back. Alice didn't really know how—she'd never fully understand it—but she *knew* she'd rescued him. When she'd chased the Black Dog of Depression—only a few hours before. When she'd added her laughter and *Brilliant*s to the laughter and *Brilliant*s of all the other kids, she'd gotten rid of the Dog and saved Luke.

She looked across at her mam. She was laughing, and crying, wiping tears from her face. Like Alice.

The phone rang. Her mother picked it up.

"Hello?"

She smiled across at Alice and whispered, "It's someone called Paddy."

"Oooh!" said one of the sausages. "Alice has a boyfriend."

"Really?" said the other sausage. "Is he a pig too?"

"Shut up, you," said Alice, and she grinned.

She'd never really spoken to a sausage before.

Suzie looked up at the sky. She was on O'Connell Street. Just hours before—but it seemed like years ago, like another life—she'd run across O'Connell Street, past the Spire, with all the other kids, chasing after the Black Dog. Now, she was back—with her mother.

She looked up and saw no clouds. None at all. The sky was a beautiful, summer-is-coming blue.

They were watching the Paddy's Day parade, with six hundred thousand other people. Coming into town for the parade had been her mother's idea. There were thousands and thousands of other kids, with their parents and other adults. Suzie recognized some of them.

They smiled back at her, secretly.

Suzie pointed up at the sky, secretly.

One of the kids looked up, and another. And another. Thousands of kids looked up at the sky, and laughed.

"What's so funny?" Suzie's mother asked.

"There's no dog in the sky," said Suzie.

Ernie was wiping the sand and dog guts off his shiny vampire shoes. He'd washed his cape and it was drying beside the fire.

Saint Paddy's Day was a national holiday, but Ernie was heading out to work.

It would be dark soon; the day was nearly over. He'd slept a bit, outside in the shed with Fang. He was feeling fine, but a bit lonely. The house was quiet. His parents were sleeping, he thought; he wasn't sure. The house was always quiet these days. Too quiet. Even Fang's farts were quiet.

Ernie didn't mind going out to work. Being a vampire took skill and determination. It wasn't for everyone. And Ernie had only recently realized: He had both skill and determination, and he loved the taste of warm blood. He had the makings of a world-class vampire. He was ambitious. There'd be films about Ernie.

"I'll knock your man Dracula off his perch," he said. "That right, Fang?"

Fang thumped the floor with his tail.

But Ernie didn't like working alone; that was the problem. He'd really enjoyed hunting the Dog, the night before. Being with all those kids for hours—he'd loved it. The chat and the messing. And what they'd done, getting rid of the Dog. That had been great too.

"D'you want to come with me tonight, Fang?" he asked.

Fang didn't thump the floor.

"Too lazy, Fang?"

Fang thumped the floor.

"Good man, Ernie."

Ernie looked up. It was his da, at the door. Ernie hadn't seen him in days. He hadn't seen him smiling in years. But he was smiling now.

"Are you headin' out to work?" his da asked.

"Yeah," said Ernie. "They won't be expecting me on a bank holiday."

"They're in for a fright, so," said Ernie's da. "Where are you headin'?"

"I thought I'd give Kilbarrack a go," said Ernie.

He was looking at his da's face, and he was suddenly very happy. Because his da was looking back at Ernie, listening to him, smiling at him—interested.

"I looked it up on Google Vampires," said Ernie. "There's a lot of blood-filled oul' ones out there."

"D'you know wha'?" said his da.

"Wha'?"

"I might come with you," said Ernie's da.

"Serious?" said Ernie.

"Yeah," said his da. "Why not? I'm sick of mopin' around. I'll go upstairs and get me cape."

He stopped at the door.

"And, Ernie?" he said.

"Wha'?"

"You're great."

"So are you, Da," said Ernie.

"Ah, now," said his da.

They looked at each other.

"We'll make a great team," said Ernie's da.

"The Blood-Suckin' O'Driscolls," said Ernie.

His da laughed.

So did Ernie.

"D'you want to come now, Fang?" he said.

Fang thumped his tail.

The zookeeper was doing his rounds, pulling a trolley, bringing dinner to all the animals. It was the same thing, the same routine, every evening.

He stopped.

He suddenly knew—he suddenly remembered. He loved it. It had been a beautiful day. It felt like the first real day of spring. The sky still looked as if it had just been painted. The animals and the birds were growling and cawing, chirping and bellowing. The way he heard it now, he thought they were calling to him.

"Coming!" he roared.

He started to pull the trolley again. It felt weightless, even though it was full.

There was a feeling in his throat. It felt familiar, although he hadn't felt it in a long time—months, a year, even longer. He knew what it was: the urge to sing.

So he sang.

"IN DUBLIN'S FAIR CIT-EEEE—"

That sounded good, he thought. He hadn't a bad little voice, if he did say so himself. So he kept singing, louder. He wanted the animals to hear.

"WHERE THE GIRRRRLS ARE SO PRETT-EEE—

"I FIRST SET MY EYES—"

He was pulling the trolley past the meerkats when he heard another voice, joining in.

"ON SWEET MOLLY MAHHH-LONE—"

He looked around but saw no one. But the other voice was still singing along with him. It was a high voice, but male.

"AS SHE WHEELED HER WHEEL BARR-OWWWW—

"THROUGH STREETS BROAD AND NARR-OW-WW—"

The zookeeper looked over the wall, into the meerkat enclosure, and saw one of the meerkats, his eyes closed, little paw on his chest, singing.

"My God!" said the zookeeper. "You can sing!"

The meerkat opened his eyes and looked up at the zookeeper.

"My God!" said Kevin. "So can you!"

And they sang together.

"CRYING COCKLES AND MUSSELS—

"ALIVE, ALIVE—OOOOOOOH."

Then they both heard a pink voice.

"Quiet over there—hellohhoh?"

People still felt depressed sometimes.

Of course, they did. It was natural. They felt good, they felt bad. They laughed, they cried. They woke, they slept. They walked, they sat. They lived, they died.

They laughed.

Times were hard, and stayed hard for a long time. But the people of Dublin still laughed, although sometimes—often—it wasn't easy.

The children knew now that they had power. They smiled their secret smiles when they met, and they pointed up at the sky. When they saw a cloud, a big dark one starting to form, they gathered together—just a few of them— and shouted "Brilliant."

Sometimes, though, they permitted the clouds to visit Dublin and rain, for days. The water was needed, and the tourists expected it.

So did the dogs.

"Will it ever, like, stop raining?" said Sadie.

"Probably not," said Chester.

"It's flattening my fur," said Sadie. "Oh my God."

"It suits you," said Chester.

They sat together outside the empty house, where that man, Ben Kelly, had lived. There was no one living there now. The grass was high. The paint on the front door was cracked. If a house could look sad, this one did. Especially in the rain.

"Look," said Sadie. "Visitors."

A van pulled up outside the house. They watched as the two children jumped out, the ones who called Ben "Uncle Ben."

"Hi, dogs," said the one that was a girl.

Then Ben got out. He smiled at the dogs, and dashed around in the wet to the back of the van. He opened it and took out a cardboard box.

He carried the box past Sadie and Chester, to the front door of the house. It was raining heavily and the box was already damp. The children followed him, running to get out of the rain. The boy patted Chester's wet head as he passed.

Ben balanced the box in one arm as he searched in a pocket for his key.

"He's coming home," Sadie whispered.

"Looks like it," said Chester.

He shrugged.

He liked those children.

Ben found the key just as the bottom of the box split open and everything in it dropped to the wet cement.

The laughter was like an explosion. Three human voices shook the whole street.

"Deadly!"

"I'm an eejit," laughed Ben.

"Yes, he is," said Chester.

They watched the humans go into the house. They heard the laughter from inside.

"Now's, like, probably a good time to tell you," said Sadie.

"What?"

"You're going to be a daddy."

Dogs don't smile or laugh.

So Chester barked instead.

ABOUT THE AUTHOR

RODDY DOYLE is an internationally acclaimed novelist, screenwriter, and playwright. In 1993, he won the Man Booker Prize for *Paddy Clarke Ha Ha Ha*. He has also published many books for children, the most recent of which, *A Greyhound of a Girl*, was short-listed for the CILIP Carnegie Medal. He lives in Dublin. He wrote this novel, a love letter to the city, in honor of its Saint Patrick's Day celebration.

ABOUT THE ILLUSTRATOR

EMILY HUGHES was born in Hawaii but now lives in England. Her picture book debut, *Wild*, was on many "best of" lists for 2014.